Dear Reader,

A few years ago I came across a fascinating book by nonfiction author Susan Casey. *The Devil's Teeth* chronicles her visits to the Farallon Islands, a National Wildlife Refuge best known for its great white sharks. Her chilling account of this extreme, isolated location sparked a story idea of my own. In the summer of 2008, when I traveled to San Francisco for the RWA National Conference, I made plans to see the islands with my agent. We braved damp weather, rough seas and a crowded charter boat. It was an unforgettable experience!

Using the Farallones as my backdrop, I sat down to write *Stranded With Her Ex,* a story about facing fears and overcoming obstacles. Although this is an unusual setting for a romance, cold and inhospitable, it is here that my characters find love again. Hearts thaw and sleeping bags heat up. I hope you enjoy the journey.

Warmest regards,

Jill Sorenson

* * *

JILL SORENSON

Stranded With Her Ex

ROMANTIC
SUSPENSE

Recycling programs
for this product may
not exist in your area.

ISBN-13: 978-0-373-27724-7

STRANDED WITH HER EX

Printed in U.S.A.

Books by Jill Sorenson

Romantic Suspense

Dangerous to Touch #1518
Stranded With Her Ex #1654

JILL SORENSON

writes sexy romantic suspense for Harlequin Books and Bantam. Her books have appeared in Cosmopolitan magazine.

After earning a degree in literature and a bilingual teaching credential from California State University, she decided teaching wasn't her cup of tea. She started writing one day while her firstborn was taking a nap and hasn't stopped since. She lives in San Diego with her husband and two young daughters.

To my agent, Laurie McLean,
for booking the charter boat to the Farallones,
and for getting the Dramamine. You are my lifesaver.

To my editor, Stacy Boyd,
for tweeting about how much you loved this story,
and for your unwavering enthusiasm.

To my husband,
my rock, who loves me for better or for worse.

To my daughters.
I couldn't have written a story about loss
without acknowledging what I've gained.
I love you both with all my heart.

To my mom, as always, for reading to me.

Chapter 1

Daniela Flores tightened her grip on the cold, wet aluminum railing. Keeping her eyes on the horizon and her feet planted on the deck, she took a series of calming breaths.

She wasn't seasick. She'd been on smaller boats in rougher water than this more times than she could count. The San Francisco Bay wasn't known for smooth sailing, and many of the other passengers were feeling poorly, but Daniela's discomfort had nothing to do with a rocking hull, unsteady surface or brisk salt spray.

Her ailment was more mental than physical. Since the accident, she disliked cramped quarters and confined spaces.

Across the crowded cabin, past whey-faced day-trippers and sturdy-legged sailors, the open sea beckoned, mocking her with its infinite expanse. Although a boat this size wasn't as restrictive as the crushed cab of a car, neither did it offer a convenient escape route. The water below was a chilly fifty degrees.

She much preferred the cool blue waves of San Diego, her hometown, where ocean temps hovered at an agreeable seventy degrees. Or southern Mexico, her birthplace, where the sea was as warm and sultry as a hot summer night.

Here, the cold water wasn't even the greatest deterrent for swimmers. Her destination, twenty-seven miles off the coast of San Francisco, was a seldom-visited place called the Farallon Islands, an infamous feeding ground for great white sharks.

The captain's intercom crackled with distortion as he made an announcement. "Devil's Teeth, dead ahead."

The Farallones had earned this moniker a hundred years ago from the fishermen and egg collectors who dared eke out a living here. With no docking facilities, the rocky crags were inhospitable to the extreme, rising from the sea in a jumble of sharp, serrated edges. Although teeming with animal life, every nook and cranny filled with birds and seals and sea lions, the surface area was devoid of greenery.

During the spring, the islands were grassy and lush, dotted with small shrubs and speckled with wildflowers. Now, in late September, the salt-sprayed granite was noticeably bare, picked as clean as old bones.

Daniela watched the godforsaken place materialize before her with a mixture of dread and anticipation. On this cold, gray day, the islands were shrouded by fog, cloaked in mystery. If anything, the landscape was even less appealing than the pictures she'd seen. And yet, she could make out the pale brown coat of a Steller sea lion, the subject of her current research project. He was reclining near the top of a cliff like a king lording over his realm.

Her heart began to race with excitement, thudding in her

chest. The Farallones were a wildlife researcher's dream come true. Surely she could set aside her phobia and enjoy her stay here. Six weeks of uninterrupted study were almost impossible to come by, and she'd been waiting over a year for this unique opportunity.

Whenever she was feeling closed in, she could do her breathing exercises. She would stay focused on the present, rather than letting the trauma of the past overwhelm her, blurring the edges of her vision and squeezing the air from her lungs. She would keep her eyes on the horizon and her feet on the ground.

As they drew closer to Southeast Farallon, the main island, she noticed a single house. It was a large, ramshackle dwelling, built over a century ago for light keepers and their families. The old Victorian stood stark and lonely on the only flat stretch of terrain, an ordinary structure on alien landscape. Like a gas station on the moon.

"They say it's haunted."

The deckhand's voice startled her. She dragged her gaze from the whitewashed house to his wind-chafed face. "The entire island?"

"Nah," he said with a smile. "Just the house."

She cast a speculative glance at the simple, no-frills structure. It was the least intimidating feature on the island. And she, like most scientists, didn't believe in ghosts. If she had, she might have believed in an afterlife, as well. Faith was a comfort she'd been denied in her darkest hour, and she wasn't going to start being superstitious now.

"I'm more worried about the sharks," she admitted.

The deckhand grunted his response and jerked his chin toward the shore. "They'll be coming for you now."

She caught a glimpse of two dark figures walking along a footpath etched into the side of the cliff, a few hundred yards from the house. With no docking facilities, setting foot on the island was a tricky process. The research biologists had access to a beat-up old Boston whaler, hoisted above the surface of the water by a formidable-looking crane.

At fifteen feet, the boat was smaller than a full-grown great white.

While she watched, one of the figures boarded the whaler, and the other lowered it to the pounding surf below. In a few efficient moments, the boat was speeding out to pick her up.

"Don't panic," she whispered, squaring her shoulders.

The man driving the boat brought it alongside the charter and killed the engine, exchanging a friendly greeting with a crew member.

When he stood, throwing the deckhand a rope to tie off the whaler, she studied him with unabashed curiosity. His legs were covered by dark, waterproof trousers and knee-high rubber boots, same as hers. Unlike her immaculate, just-purchased ensemble, his clothes were well-used and far from spotless. His jacket was splotched with what might have been bird droppings, and his face was shadowed by a week's worth of stubble.

"Seen any sharks today?" the deckhand asked.

The man grinned. "Day ain't over yet."

Based on his dark good looks, she guessed that this was Jason Ruiz, the Filipino oceanographer she'd been communicating with via email. She'd seen a grainy photo of him once and it hadn't done him justice.

The deckhand lobbed her duffel in his direction. After catching it deftly, Jason motioned with his gloved fingers. "Toss her to me. I'm ready."

The deckhand's eyes were merry, full of mischief.

Daniela took a step back. "I'd rather not—"

"We're just messing with you," Jason said, patting the aluminum seat beside him. "Jump over here."

She moistened her lips, measuring the distance between the boats with trepidation. The expanse was less than two feet, but the drop went quite a ways down. And, although the whaler was tied off, it was still a moving target.

Her stomach churned as she watched it pitch and sway. "Jump?"

"Yeah. And try not to hit water. Just because we haven't seen the sharks doesn't mean they aren't there."

The deckhand laughed, as if this were a joke. It wasn't. This time of year, the sharks were most definitely there. They came to the Farallones every fall to dine on a rich assortment of seals and sea lions.

Daniela stared at the surface of the water, feeling faint.

She'd been briefed about the boat situation, of course. But reading a matter-of-fact description detailing the steps needed to access the island was different than actually going through with it. Leaping from a charter to an aluminum boat in shark-infested waters was madness. One false move, one tiny miscalculation, and...

Gulp.

Jason gave the deckhand a knowing smirk. "Just throw her to me, Jackie. She can't weigh much more than that bag."

"No," she protested, taking a step forward. She was pretty sure they were teasing again, but she also didn't want to give herself time to reconsider. Chickening out before she'd begun was not an option.

She took a deep breath and grabbed Jason's proffered hand, hopping over the short but frightening precipice.

She didn't fall into the water. She didn't hit the aluminum seat, either. She collided with Jason Ruiz, almost knocking them both off balance. He threw his arms around her and braced his legs wide, holding her steady until the boat stopped rocking.

Daniela clung to him, her heart racing. She hadn't been this close to a man in a long time, and it felt good. Strange, but good. He was much taller than she was, and a lot stronger. She could feel the muscles in his arms and the flatness of his chest against her breasts.

He smelled good, too. Like salt and ocean and hard work. But even while she registered these sensations, there was one irrational, overriding thought: *He's not Sean.*

"I'm sorry," she said, clearing her throat.

"Don't mention it," he murmured, making sure she was ready to stand on her own before he released her. "I never get tired of beautiful women throwing themselves at me. I only wish I'd showered in recent memory." The corner of his mouth tipped up. "There's a shortage of hot water on the island, and we're all a bit rank."

She couldn't help but smile. "You don't smell bad."

"Really? I thought I smelled like bird crap and B.O."

Laughing, she shook her head. "Bird crap, maybe." The faint odor of ammonia filled her nostrils, but it was coming from the island, not him.

"I'm Jason."

"Daniela," she said, grasping his hand. As quickly as it came, the sexual tension between them dissolved. He was still smiling at her in an appreciative, masculine way, and she was smiling back at him, unable to deny his considerable appeal, but there was no intensity to their mutual admiration.

With his easy charm and handsome face, he probably had a way with the ladies. She'd known men like him before. Her ex-husband, for one. Women had always dropped at Sean's feet, and he'd done little to discourage them.

Feeling her smile slip, she pulled her hand away.

If he noticed her change of mood, he didn't remark upon it. "Ready?" he asked, catching the rope the deckhand threw at him and tucking it away.

Nodding, she perched on the edge of the aluminum seat, paralyzed by self-consciousness. She was so far out of her element here. The past two years, she'd been in virtual seclusion, working from her desk at home and putting in late hours at the research facility. She'd interacted with more spreadsheets than animals. This trip was, in part, an attempt to get her life back. A return to her roots.

She hadn't chosen conservation biology to spend all her time indoors.

Rubbing elbows with other scientists, most of whom were men, was nothing new, and she was no stranger to roughing it, but she hadn't socialized, much less dated, in ages. The close proximity of a hot guy rattled her more than she'd like to admit.

And she couldn't stop comparing him to Sean.

The two men probably knew each other. There weren't that many shark experts in the world, let alone the West Coast, and Jason was from San Diego. They were close in age, although Sean was about five years older. Both of them were tall and fit and remarkably good-looking. They were also consummate outdoorsmen and staunch environmentalists, more comfortable on a surfboard than in a boardroom.

Upon closer inspection, Jason was the more striking of the two, with his dark eyes and sensual mouth. But Sean's all-American ruggedness had always hit her in the right spot.

Daniela turned her gaze back to the calm-inducing horizon. She hadn't seen Sean in over a year, but he still managed to monopolize her thoughts.

Jason maneuvered the whaler into position beneath the

boom, a task that required concentration and dexterity. When he found the right place, he stood and hitched the heavy metal hook to the hull with no assistance from Daniela.

She did her best to hang on to her seat and stay out of his way.

Once connected, the whaler was lifted high into the air by the crane, and this ride was no less nerve-wracking than the two-hour boat trip to the islands or the precarious jump she'd taken a few moments ago. She gripped the aluminum bench until her knuckles went white. When the boat shuddered to a stop over dry land, she breathed a sigh of relief and flexed her icy hands.

She couldn't believe she was actually here. Southeast Farallon Island was an odd place, like no other on earth, and the first thing that struck her was the noise. It was nature in chaos. The sound of crashing surf and cawing birds reverberated in her ears, and wind whipped at her clothes, like children vying for attention.

Jason grinned at the boom operator, clearly at home in this wild place. "Thanks, Liz," he shouted, raising his voice to be heard above the cacophony.

The woman at the controls watched while Jason helped Daniela climb from the dangling boat, her expression cool.

Daniela stepped forward to introduce herself. "Liz? I'm Daniela Flores."

"Elizabeth Winters," she said, extending a slender, black-gloved hand.

Daniela accepted her handshake with an uncertain smile.

"I'm the only one allowed to call her Liz," Jason explained, hefting the duffel bag over his shoulder. "Because we're special friends."

Elizabeth regarded him like he was something unpleasant stuck to the bottom of her shoe. Daniela didn't know what to make of her. She was tall and slim, dressed in weatherproof fabric from head to toe, with a gray-blue windbreaker that matched the color of her eyes. A thick auburn braid trailed over one shoulder, and she had the delicate skin of a redhead. Her face was pale and freckled and very lovely.

"I'll refrain from sharing my pet name for you," she said drily.

He laughed, delighted to have irked her. Elizabeth seemed more annoyed than amused. Perhaps she was immune to charming men.

Daniela decided that she liked her. "How is your conservation project coming along?" she asked as they followed Jason down the steep, pebble-strewn path toward the house. "I was fascinated by the study you published recently on the black-feathered cormorant."

Elizabeth's cheeks flushed with pleasure. "Thank you. The islands get so much attention for their sharks." She made a face at Jason's well-formed back, as if he were responsible for the Farallones' notoriety. "Many of the birds here are more unique, and in far greater need of protection, but the majority of funding is spent on shark research. Investors with deep pockets love to see red water and flashing teeth."

"Watch your step," Jason reminded, turning toward Elizabeth and placing his hand on her slim waist.

She tensed at his touch. "I'm fine."

Nodding, he released her and continued on.

Daniela traversed the slope with caution, feeling rocks crumble and roll like ball bearings beneath her booted feet.

"Where was I?" Elizabeth asked.

"'Flashing teeth,'" Daniela supplied, eyes cast downward.

"Oh, right. The tourists come for the sharks as well. Boatloads of gawkers cruise by every weekend. I mean, this is supposed to be an animal sanctuary. Last Sunday they all but ruined my chances at seeing two blue-crested warblers mate—"

Her rising voice shut off like a switch as she lost her footing. Quick as lightning, Jason caught her by both arms and hauled her against him, saving her from a nasty tumble down the side of the cliff.

She stared up at him, wide-eyed and short of breath.

"Like I said," he murmured, letting her go. "Watch your step."

"Sorry." With a trilling laugh, she glanced back at Daniela. "I tend to get overexcited, talking about my causes."

"No need to apologize for being passionate," Daniela said, intrigued by the subject matter. Not to mention the byplay between Elizabeth and Jason. "How close do the tourists get?" she asked as they started down the hill again. "I thought the waters here were too treacherous for recreational boaters."

"Oh, they are," Jason replied. "But a cage-diving operation comes during shark season. They dock a couple of hundred feet offshore, drop the cages and throw out chum."

Daniela was shocked. "They *chum?* Near the islands?" The practice of throwing out shark bait, a noxious mixture of blood and fish parts, was looked down on by scientists. It changed the animals' natural behavior and made them less wary of humans.

"Yeah. It's not illegal."

She arrived at the base of the slope, where the ground

was more stable. "I can't imagine getting in the water here. Even with a steel cage for protection."

"Crazy thrill seekers," Jason said, winking at Elizabeth. Obviously, his profession as a shark researcher put him in the same category. "Daniela is here to observe the Steller sea lion. She's from the Scripps Institute in San Diego."

Elizabeth's brows rose. "Excellent. That's a top-notch organization."

"Oh, yes," Daniela said, unable to contain her own excitement. "We're collecting the necessary data to keep the Steller on the endangered list. I hope my work here makes a difference."

"So do I," Elizabeth said kindly.

"We've got an awesome crew this season." Jason shifted the weight of her duffel as he approached the front door of the house. "Brent Masterson is here, filming some footage for his documentary. Taryn Evans is one of the most enthusiastic interns I've ever met. And although Dr. Fitzwilliam had to back out at the last minute, his replacement is a name I'm sure you'll recognize. We've snagged the leading shark expert in the Western Hemisphere—"

Daniela's stomach dropped as soon as he opened the door. For, standing behind it was a man she recognized very well, indeed. The leading shark expert of the Western Hemisphere had his hands all over a gorgeous blonde, laughing as he tried to wrestle her to the ground.

"—Sean Carmichael," Jason finished, gazing upon Daniela's ex-husband with hero-worship in his eyes.

Chapter 2

Sean disentangled himself from the young woman quickly, his face going slack. The football the pair had been grappling over dropped to the threadbare rug with a solid thud.

Still laughing, the girl picked it up off the floor and straightened, running a hand through her long, wavy hair.

Daniela hated her immediately.

"I'm Taryn," the girl said, a dimple appearing in her sunny cheek.

"Daniela," she murmured in response, managing a limp handshake. She felt bloodless, as though her spirit had been drained from her, sucked out by the island wind and taken far away, across the turbulent sea.

Why was Sean here? He was supposed to be in Baja California. She'd checked.

An uncomfortable silence, punctuated by the ticking

of a clock on the far wall, seemed to stretch out into an eternity. Jason looked back and forth between Daniela and Sean, puzzled by the tension in the room. "Do you two know each other?"

Sean recovered first. He'd always been quick on his feet. "She's my ex-wife," he said, explaining their relationship in the same tone he'd have used to mention a vague professional connection. He gave her a polite nod. "Hello, Daniela."

Although it took an effort, she inclined her head, acknowledging him in the same detached manner. "Sean."

Taryn nibbled on her lush lower lip, as if trying to figure out if Daniela's presence meant her fun and games with Sean were over.

Jason also seemed to be considering the ramifications. "Is there a problem?"

"Yes," Sean said.

"No," said Daniela at the same time.

Jason frowned. "She doesn't have a restraining order against you or anything, does she?"

Sean shot him a dark look, insulted by the suggestion that a woman would require protection from him. "Of course not."

Accepting the answer without question, Jason turned his attention back to Daniela, a hint of regret in his eyes. Being a lowly seal researcher, rather than a leading shark expert, she was the more dispensable of the two.

Her mood plummeted. She didn't need a weather diagram to know which way the wind blew on Farallon Island. Sean was a superstar in this field, and his unscheduled visit here was a coup. Compared to him, she was nobody. Jason Ruiz wouldn't care how pretty she was if Sean wanted her gone.

She forced herself to meet Sean's eyes. "Can we talk outside?"

"Sure," he muttered, grabbing a jacket off the dilapidated couch in the living room. On his way out, he exchanged a glance with Taryn, conveying a silent, intimate message that cut Daniela to the quick.

Taryn watched them depart with undisguised interest.

Daniela walked about a dozen steps from the house and stopped, hugging her arms around her body. Because the island was covered by sharp rocks, kamikaze seagulls and 5,000-pound elephant seals, it was no place to take a leisurely stroll.

At least the wind would make their conversation impossible to overhear. It blew her hair in every direction, whipping the shoulder-length strands against her cheeks.

She stared out at the horizon, collecting her thoughts. Although she disliked being at Sean's mercy, she'd have to suck it up and make nice. There was so much riding on this project. Her career, the cause…her peace of mind, even. In a way, she'd come here to find herself.

She'd been lost for so long.

Spending time on a deserted island with her ex-husband wasn't going to be easy, but she was a survivor. She'd lived through worse than this. Compared to some of the other challenges she'd faced in her life, his presence was a minor roadblock.

They'd been married for more than five years; surely they could put up with each other for a few short weeks.

"You look good," he said, after a long moment.

Surprised by the compliment, she turned to face him.

"Your hair is longer," he added unnecessarily. "And you seem…" His gaze dropped to her breasts, which were impossible to hide, even in a boxy windbreaker. "Healthier," he muttered, a flush creeping up his neck.

If he meant to flatter her, he was off base. After the accident, she'd cropped her hair short, and in the following year she'd lost a lot of weight. She'd overheard him telling his best friend that she resembled a scrawny boy.

One careless remark, never discussed, never repeated, but it had damaged their already strained relationship. The last thing she needed was a reminder that he liked long, luscious hair and generous curves.

Sexist pig.

He was looking a bit rawboned himself, but she didn't say that. Lean or not, he was the picture of health. Shedding a few pounds only made his shoulders appear broader and his face more angular. Underneath his clothes, she knew he would be perfectly cut, all lovely muscles etched into sun-bronzed flesh.

Beautiful bastard.

His hair was longer, too, curling at the edge of his collar, as if he'd been too busy to have it trimmed. He hadn't bothered to shave in a few days, either. His whiskers appeared thicker than ever, but she knew from experience that they would feel soft to the touch. Her fingertips tingled at the memory of exploring his stubbly jaw and hard mouth. Both were deceptively rough-looking.

She resisted the absurd longing to lift her hand to his face. "I need this," she said in a low voice.

Sean shook his head. "You don't belong here, Dani. It's too harsh, too volatile. You're…not equipped."

"That isn't fair," she said. "You haven't even seen me since—"

"When's the last time you had an anxiety attack?" he interrupted.

Crossing her arms over her chest, she studied the horizon instead of him. Breathe, she reminded herself. Just breathe.

"A month ago? A week?"

"I can handle it." He'd witnessed her worst breakdowns, so she couldn't blame him for being concerned. She could, however, resent him for treating her like an invalid, and for thinking she was weak. "I'm stronger now."

His eyes wandered over her face. "Are you?"

"Yes! You really think that teenybopper you were playing full-contact with is tougher than I am? After all I've been through?"

"She's twenty-four."

Jealousy burned within her, hot and bright. "Did you interrogate her this way, too? Make sure she was mentally fit?"

"I didn't have to. She's very…easygoing."

Daniela choked out a laugh. Nothing he could have said would hurt more. Compared to her, everyone seemed easy. "How perfect for you."

He didn't disagree.

She pushed the pain of his betrayal aside, searching for the right words to convince him. "I've been on the waiting list for over a year, Sean. Don't take this opportunity away from me because you came out here on a whim. Please."

He shifted from one foot to the other, his face taut. "There's been an incident."

"What kind of incident?"

"Someone skinned a seal pup."

The breath rushed from her lungs. "When?"

"A few days ago. We found it on the north side."

Daniela blinked a few times, struggling to understand. "The body washed up?"

"No. It was fresh."

"That's impossible! The island is virtually inaccessible."

He inclined his head in agreement. "Virtually."

"Who would do that?"

"Maybe a disgruntled fisherman, or a member of the cage-diving crew. Either way, it's been damned odd around here lately. We're all on edge. The last thing I want is for you to come across some crazy…anti-environmentalist." He was quiet for a moment, his gaze searching hers. "I don't want you to get hurt."

A lump rose to her throat. She swallowed hard, thinking she'd much rather deal with his criticism than his tenderness. "I won't," she promised, her voice huskier than usual. "I appreciate your concern, but I can't run away at the first sign of trouble. I need to face my fears, Sean. I came here to move on."

His eyes darkened with a sharp, indefinable emotion. She knew the situation was difficult for him, too. Much of what had gone wrong between them had been her fault; she'd given up on their marriage long before he had.

And when she realized her mistake, it had been too late.

The radio under his jacket crackled with disturbance. "Shark attack, southwest side. Near Skull Rock. Looks like a big one."

It was a man's voice, one she didn't recognize. Sean unclipped his radio and responded with an affirmative, glancing up toward the lighthouse. Beside it, there was a lone figure, waving his arms in the direction of the attack.

Jason flew out of the house, a digital video camera in his hands, his open jacket flapping behind him. There was no more time for negotiation. "Who's with me?" he said, heading toward the landing.

It went without saying that Sean was. He lived for this.

He started after Jason, following him away from the

house. Daniela had to jog to keep up with his long strides. The man at the lighthouse tower also hurried down the path, eager to accompany them.

"Sure you want to see this?" Sean asked over his shoulder. "It's a bloody mess."

As soon as he spoke those words, she was assaulted by images from another disturbing scene. Shrieking metal and shattered glass. The warm, wet rush of blood and the agonizing pain spreading through her belly.

"Yes," she said anyway, fighting to clear her mind of memories. This was a test, like jumping from boat to boat, and failure was not an option. Heart racing, she scrambled along behind him, her feet seeking purchase on the rocky soil.

He should have checked the roster before signing on.

It had never occurred to Sean that his ex-wife would be on the list of researchers. Southeast Farallon was the last place on earth she should be.

He was glad she'd decided to return to the world of the living, but this wasn't it. In fact, native Californians had called the Farallones "The Islands of the Dead." The conditions were too extreme for someone who'd gone through what she had.

It was like tossing a soldier with PTSD into a battle demonstration. Only, this was no demonstration.

Maybe after witnessing a twenty-foot shark decapitate an elephant seal, she'd go back to the mainland on the next charter. He hoped so. It wasn't as if he didn't wish her the best. It was just that the best thing for her was to be somewhere else.

Somewhere peaceful.

She didn't need to rub her face in carnage to prove to

him, or anyone, that she could handle the sight of blood again.

When they all loaded into the whaler, Jason passed the handheld camera to Sean and got behind the wheel. Brent, who'd managed to grab his own video equipment, settled in across from Daniela, and Sean took the space beside her.

Elizabeth operated the crane, lowering them down to the surface of the water.

"You must be Daniela," Brent said, offering her his hand. "I'm Brent Masterson."

"Pleased to meet you."

Although her smile was bland, he scanned her face with undisguised interest, recording every line and angle. Sean knew he was thinking that Daniela would look great on camera. Her big brown eyes and captivating features made her spectacularly photogenic.

As soon as the boat touched the surface, Jason unhooked the chain and revved up the engine, speeding toward Skull Rock.

Sean passed the handheld camera to Daniela. "Film."

Her cheeks paled. "What?"

"I tag," Sean said. "Jason drives. You and Brent can film."

"You're going to tag it?"

He nodded. "I need my hands free."

Tagging was a quick, easy process, and Sean could have filmed himself, but getting Daniela behind the lens would be good for her. It was a task to focus on, a small insulation, one step removed from the horror.

"B-be careful," she mumbled, lifting the video camera to her face.

Even in a state of shock and uncertainty, she was breathtaking. Being with her again was a jolt to his system, as powerful and disturbing as the first time he'd set eyes on her. He remembered that day with perfect clarity.

She'd been hurrying toward the parking lot at San Diego State, a stack of textbooks under one arm, a sleek leather tote bag in the other. With her stylish clothes and arresting good looks, she was a world apart from the granola girls he usually gravitated toward.

One glimpse of her, and his heart had stalled in his chest.

He was a post-grad student, teaching his first class, and if he hadn't already been late he'd have followed her. As it was, he'd turned to watch her go, ogling her in a way that was gauche and obvious and embarrassingly impolite.

Maybe it was fate, because she showed up in his classroom a few minutes later. Apparently, she'd forgotten the syllabus and had gone back to her car to retrieve it.

He was sure he'd babbled nonsense for most of the hour, but she hadn't seemed to mind. In fact, she'd approached him after, claiming to have enjoyed his lecture. Every time the class met after that, she sat closer to the front of the room.

During the final exam she'd been in the first row, wearing a low-cut top so distracting he'd stuttered whenever his eyes tripped over her.

That was ten years ago.

He didn't know how they'd arrived at this painful juncture, and it hurt too much to retrace the steps. Trying to live without her the past year had been agony for him, but it hadn't been as bad as living with her, watching her slip away.

Was she truly on the mend?

He hadn't lied when he'd told her she looked good. She was lovelier than ever, to be honest. The new hairstyle worked for her, framing her heart-shaped face and feathering out against her cheeks, drawing his attention to her mouth.

He wished he didn't remember all the things she'd done to him with it.

Pulling his gaze away from her, he searched the horizon, looking for a seal carcass or a boil on the surface of the water. The tearing motion great whites used while feeding, tails whipping back and forth, created a unique disturbance.

Skull Rock, the islands' most striking natural feature, loomed in the near distance. While most of the rock formations were jagged, jutting toward the sky like a row of wicked teeth, the Skull had a rounded shape and two distinctive, cavernous indentations. One went all the way through to the other side, giving the impression of a gaping eye socket.

It was a fitting place for a kill.

Jason saw the body before he did. "Starboard side, twenty meters," he said, cutting the boat's speed to a crawl.

Daniela turned her head, doing a visual sweep of the area.

Sean placed his hand on her shoulder. "There," he said, pointing her in the right direction. She was trembling, and that would affect the video, but it hardly mattered. He'd taken some shaky footage himself.

A certain amount of fear was normal. Hell, if you weren't scared of a lightning-quick predator with razor-sharp teeth and the striking power of a Mack truck, something was fundamentally wrong with you.

Of course, the shark was nowhere to be seen at the moment. Only the headless body of a California sea lion was visible, floating in a slick red bath. The water wouldn't keep the color long, for the Pacific Ocean was a vast expanse, but while the animal bled out it was surrounded by a shock of crimson, pure and dark and undiluted.

"Wh-where is it?" Daniela whispered, camera focused on the corpse.

"Close by," he said, dropping his hand from her shoulder. He wanted to keep touching her, to make sure she stayed put. Which was foolish, as no one in their right mind would leap from a boat in this situation. "Zoom in."

She fumbled with the camera for a moment, familiarizing herself with the controls before she resumed filming. Her face was pale and drawn, her eyes stark.

Brent attached his underwater camera to a pole with a crooked arm and lowered it into the water. He didn't talk much while he was filming, claiming that the man behind the lens shouldn't be seen *or* heard.

Next to him, Jason Ruiz was silent at the helm. Although he was more loquacious than Brent, he knew shark behavior as well as Sean, and kept his comments to a minimum while they were out here. He was a good scientist, if a little overeager, and they got on well.

When Jason glanced up at Sean now, his eyes narrowed for a split second before he looked away.

The younger man's disapproval wasn't obvious, and Sean was almost convinced he'd imagined it. Over the past few days, Jason had treated him with deference and respect and damned near adoration. It was kind of annoying, actually.

Less than an hour with Daniela, and he'd switched sides.

Jason hadn't known about their marriage, but perhaps he'd heard a few random details about the divorce. They'd separated after she almost died in a car accident, which didn't cast Sean in a very positive light. His ex-wife also had a singular effect on people, especially men, and Jason had a weakness for the ladies.

He'd never met a beautiful woman he didn't want to sleep with.

Sean could practically hear him thinking, "You dumped *her? Are you insane?* She's *hot.*"

She'd dumped him, not the other way around, but almost everyone assumed the failed relationship was his fault. They were right, in a way. He'd been unable to protect her, incapable of comforting her and at an utter loss for the right words to say to her.

"Why isn't it…eating?" she whispered, her voice wavering.

"A pause between the first strike and a feeding isn't unusual. We think they're making sure the prey is in no condition to fight back."

This sea lion wouldn't put up a fuss—not without a head. White sharks often attacked by ambush, rocketing toward the target from underneath and incapacitating it in one fatal blow. The current victim had been in the wrong place at the wrong time, swimming too far from the shallows and too close to the surface.

Although blood no longer gushed from the wound, the animal's exposed vertebra was a grisly sight, and the air was thick with the smell of death. Seabirds waited on nearby perches, feathers fluttering, ready to snap up a meaty scrap.

Sean watched Daniela's throat work as she swallowed back her nausea. She was holding up well, considering. As a marine biologist, she'd interacted with dangerous animals before. They'd worked in the field together on a regular basis, so he knew her level of expertise.

He'd seen her reach out to stroke the slippery back of a stingray, grin with delight when visited by a school of blue sharks, stand up to a braying Northern seal and get bitten on her pretty little backside as she beat a hasty retreat.

Daniela had a way with animals, a confidence gained from experience and a natural ease that couldn't be taught. She wasn't a shark expert, however, and the great whites at the Farallones were like no other predator on earth.

With her unsteady nerves and devastating personal history, she wasn't the best candidate for this kind of research.

The sight of a white shark breaching, or propelling its massive body above the surface of the water during the initial attack was heart-stopping. There was also no way to predict this occurrence, so footage of it was rare. Unlike in the movies, most sharks didn't advertise their locations by flashing fins before a bite.

Feeding frenzies were also unusual. After the kill, whites ate with economical efficiency, and they weren't the most dexterous of fish. If their movements caused the surface of the water to bubble like a pot of seafood gumbo, it was because they were powerhouses, not because they were doing underwater gymnastics.

Sean knew what to expect, but the wait always created tension. Anticipating Daniela's reaction made the situation more uneasy.

The whaler was only fifteen feet long, and it seemed to shrink as time dragged on. A patch of coastal fog settled over the upper half of the island, bringing with it an eerie quiet, a silence charged with dread and unholy glee.

At Skull Rock, beady-eyed scavengers shuffled their clawed feet.

When the shark broke through the surface of the water, Daniela startled, almost dropping the video camera. She took a series of short, quick breaths, fright apparent on her fine features, the rapid beat of her pulse visible in her slender neck.

Sean didn't need a Ph.D to diagnose her anxiety, or any special intuition to realize she was reliving the trauma of the wreck. Her face was so pale, he feared she would faint. He considered dropping the tagging equipment to offer her his assistance. Brent, whose attention should have been focused on directing the underwater camera, seemed concerned by her distress. And it went without saying that Jason was enraptured.

Just as Sean was about to call off the shoot, Daniela pulled herself together. Spine straightening, she held the video camera in a steady, if white-knuckled, grip.

The evidence of her courage caused a strange welling of emotions within him. Pride, and sadness and regret. His eyes watered and his throat closed up. How ironic, he thought, if *he* turned out to be the one who couldn't hold it together.

After a moment, the pressure in his chest eased and he was able to drag his gaze away from her. The white had moved in and was nibbling a big chunk of flesh from the decapitated sea lion's side. By the looks of it, the shark was an adult, and good-sized, too. At least eighteen or nineteen feet.

"It's Shirley," Jason said, a grin lighting across his face.

"It sure as hell is," Sean replied, returning his smile.

Shirley was a breeding female, and that was always a welcome sight at the Farallones. She had a crescent-shaped scar above her left eye, small but easy to recognize, and she was often spotted with her full-figured friend, Laverne.

The pair had been named by Sean a couple of years ago. Jason had seen them both last year, but hadn't been able to tag either. The number of great whites in the world was ever-dwindling, and the circle of shark researchers was small. Although Jason and Sean didn't know each other that well, they knew a lot of the same sharks.

They studied Shirley in reverent silence while she tore and chewed and swallowed. A flurry of greedy seagulls dogged her every movement, snatching up stringy bits of gore, wings flapping. While the effect wasn't aesthetically pleasing, the mood on the boat was no longer sinister, and any hint of animosity from Jason was gone.

Still smiling, he eased the whaler in closer.

"Wh-what are we doing?" Daniela asked, one hand reaching out to grab the edge of the hull, steadying herself.

Sean's blood turned to ice. "Keep your hands inside the boat."

"Why? It's over there."

"*One* of them is over there," he corrected, trying not to visualize Laverne breaching beside the boat, taking most of Daniela's arm with her.

She snatched her hand back. And just like that, she lost her focus. Letting the camera sag, she searched the surface of the water with terrified eyes, pressing her palm to her lower abdomen in a way that was familiar and absolutely heartbreaking.

Sean wanted to kick himself. He didn't know what he should have said differently, or what to say now to calm her down.

"Look at me," Jason said.

Gulping, she met his steady gaze.

"We're going in closer to tag her. It only takes a minute. And Sean's a pro. You know that, right?"

Her eyes darted from him to Sean. "Yeah," she said, moistening her lips.

"Good. You just keep filming. You're doing a great job."

Brent nodded helpfully. "You'll be fine."

Like a trooper, she put the camera back up to her face and resumed filming. Her movements were stiff, even robotic, but she was working through the fear, maintaining her composure and refusing to let the past overwhelm her.

He hazarded a glance at Jason, who merely shrugged and maneuvered the whaler into position. Sean should have felt grateful that someone had been coolheaded enough to help Daniela. Instead, he was sick with envy.

And Brent knew it. Sean could tell by the way he averted his eyes, turning his attention back to the surface of the water.

Unlike Jason, Sean didn't have an easy way with words. He wasn't suave, expressive or articulate. His inability to communicate his feelings to Daniela had played a major role in their breakup. And just now, his thoughtless comment had caused her panicked reaction.

By trying to keep her safe, he'd only put her in more danger.

A muscle in Sean's jaw ticked as he located the tagging equipment, clicking the various components into place with swift, angry motions. This was what he knew. Scientific gadgets and cold-blooded animals.

Here, no words were necessary.

Chapter 3

Coming here had been a mistake.

Sean was right. Daniela knew that now.

Why had she thought she was strong enough to keep her cool on a tiny aluminum boat in turbulent, shark-filled waters? She wasn't. Anyone who found this type of situation exciting, or even remotely safe, was certifiable.

The whaler they were sitting in was a joke. What would prevent one of those ferocious beasts from bumping it? One nudge, and they'd all be overboard, swimming for their lives in noxious, red-tinged water.

She almost gagged. The air smelled like a rendering plant.

What would stop Shirley from biting into the boat? A great white had some of the most powerful jaws in the animal kingdom. Those teeth could cut through the hull like it was a soda can.

Shirley had devoured a 500-pound sea lion in less than a dozen bites.

Jason and Sean had watched her chow down with identical expressions of pride on their handsome faces, grinning like the maniacs they were. Brent's demeanor was more circumspect, but no less pleased. He was getting great footage.

As they moved in closer, Daniela's unease grew. The shark was not only longer than the boat, she was wider. Her mouth gaped open, larger than the circle of Daniela's arms, ringed by rows of serrated white daggers.

This shark could swallow her whole. And that toothy grin was less than two feet from the side of the boat.

It was all she could do to keep filming while Sean stood and leaned out, tagging the shark's slippery back as easily as if he'd been giving a fellow surfer a high five.

Daniela had been fighting a breakdown for most of the day. The sight of him taking such a shocking risk, and doing it with ineffable nonchalance, almost sent her careening over the edge. Somehow, she continued to point the camera at the thing in the water, a now unrecognizable mass of shiny black flesh and red-soaked teeth. Birds swooped down around them from every direction, literally plucking strings of meat from the mouth of the monster.

Time seemed to slow down and speed up after that. One moment, they were out on the water, watching the brutality of nature, survival of the fittest in action, a violent blur of sound and motion and color. The next, they were sailing through the air, disappearing into a blanket of late-afternoon fog.

Too numb to speak, she held herself as stiff as a board while the crane lifted the whaler up to the landing.

The day was almost over, she realized with bleak

surprise. In this bizarre, uncivilized place, what would nightfall bring?

All three men were staring at her, so she took the camera away from her face, finally, and felt the world crash into sharp focus. The landscape was too foreign, too harsh for tender eyes. The sea was too dark, too blue, too vast.

"Here," she mumbled, turning off the camera and handing it to Jason.

Sean helped her out of the boat. The instant her feet hit ground, her knees buckled. "Easy," he said, steadying her. His arms felt even stronger than Jason's, and twice as disturbing. She righted herself, her face growing hot.

"When did you eat last?"

"This morning," she said, embarrassed by her shakiness, and annoyed with him for calling her on it. Worse, her body tingled from his touch. Even through layers of clothing, his hands left an imprint on her skin.

She backed up a step, bumping into Jason.

"You're in for a treat, then," he said, putting his arm around her shoulders. "It's my turn to cook. Have you ever had *lumpia?*"

She nodded. "I like it."

Jason walked forward, leading her toward the footpath. "I knew you would. The rest of the week, we have to suffer through bland, ordinary fare. On my night, we dine in style."

Her lips curved into a wobbly smile.

"Please tell me you're planning to make something spicy and Mexican and extra-delicious when it's your turn to cook."

She glanced back at Sean and Brent, who were trailing behind them. Sean seemed displeased, perhaps because Jason was acting as though he wanted her to stay. "I'm not a big fan of super-spicy food, actually. The part of Mexico

I'm from isn't known for that. But if you have the right ingredients, I can make tamales."

Jason made a murmur of interest and inquired about the recipe, keeping his hand at her waist as they continued down the hillside. If Sean had touched her this way, she'd have bristled, but with Jason, she didn't care. In a far corner of her mind, she knew he was humoring her, trying to get her to focus on mundane pleasantries rather than the nerve-jolting bloodbath they'd just witnessed.

As they reached the end of the path, the sun dipped low on the horizon, leaving the island cloaked in shadows and damp with mist. The temperature had dropped considerably, and there was a chill in the air that seemed to invade her very bones.

The inside of the house was warmer, but the creaky old Victorian had been built to withstand pounding rain and gale force winds, not for enjoying cozy nights by the fire. There was no lighted hearth, no golden glow and no central heating.

The place lacked ambiance, with its sturdy furniture and bare walls, but it had a certain dorm-room, flophouse charm. Adding to the collegiate atmosphere, Taryn was sitting at a worktable, scribbling in a notebook under the light of an antique lamp.

The sight of her sunny, California-girl beauty made Daniela's stomach twist.

Elizabeth headed upstairs, escaping any possible future drama. "I think I'll go freshen up before dinner."

"No need for formal wear," Jason said. "We're dining *en famille*."

Rolling her eyes at his lame joke, she left the room. No one in their right mind would bring anything but work clothes to Southeast Farallon.

Brent sat down on the couch by the window and began

checking his camera equipment. It registered with Daniela that he had strong, elegant hands. Sculptor's hands. He was also handsome in an understated way, with short brown hair and fine blue eyes.

In the chaos of the attack, she'd hardly noticed.

Daniela snuck another glance at Sean, feeling raw, emotional and distinctly out of place. He stared back at her, saying nothing. It was obvious that he didn't want her to stay, but she couldn't go anywhere tonight.

Jason cleared his throat. "I already put your bag in your room, Daniela. Taryn will show you the way."

The girl's chair scraped against the scarred hardwood flooring. "I'd be happy to," she said, standing.

"I think I can find it."

Taryn waved her off. "Don't be silly. I'll give you a tour."

Before Taryn and Daniela went upstairs, Sean and Jason beat a silent retreat, disappearing through the door and into the twilight. It didn't take a genius to know they were going outside to discuss her. And decide her fate.

"Come on," Taryn said, smiling as if there was nothing amiss.

Brent looked out the window, craning his neck for a glimpse of the other men and making no attempt to curb his curiosity.

With a sigh, Daniela followed Taryn, forced to stare at the girl's perky little bottom as she ascended the stairs. Taryn was tall and coltish, model-slim in her formfitting leggings and oversized sweatshirt. The same outfit would have made Daniela look like a tree stump.

"Do they always do that?" she asked.

"Do what?"

She nodded toward the front door, where Sean and Jason

had just exited. "Give each other dark, brooding looks and talk outside?"

"No," Taryn admitted. "They acted like best pals until…"

You came. Daniela knew what she'd been about to say.

Terrific. One afternoon on the island, and she was like a disease.

"This is the bathroom," Taryn said brightly, opening a door on the right side. It was small and dreary, with old-fashioned fixtures and a plain white sink. "The downstairs toilet flushes better, but this one works if you have to pee in the middle of the night. And here is the ever-popular shower." She slid open the frosted glass door, inclining her slender arm with the panache of a television model.

Daniela peered into the putty-colored stall. It wasn't fancy, but it was clean. "Jason said there's no hot water?"

"It comes and goes. Tricky pipes. We take turns and hope for the best. Sometimes I have to heat a pot of water on the stove to wash with. Of course, the boys don't seem to mind being grungy." She wrinkled her adorable, sun-kissed nose. "Soon, we'll have more rainwater. We cache it in the cistern and use it for the rest of the year."

Daniela nodded. Working in the field meant dealing with whatever conditions were available. Running water, at any temperature, was a luxury.

Taryn continued the tour, opening the first door on the left. "This is us. Brent's room is the next one down. Jason and Sean are there, on the opposite side. And Elizabeth is the last door on the right."

The room was sparsely furnished, boasting a set of bunk beds, a small desk and one ladder-backed chair. She frowned, confused by the sight of her duffel bag on the lower bunk. "This is…*our* room?"

"Yes. I hope you don't mind. Elizabeth likes to keep to herself, but I prefer having a roommate." She lowered her voice to a whisper. "Just between you and me, it gets kind of spooky around here at night."

Daniela fell silent, wondering if Sean was Taryn's preferred roommate. Maybe he wasn't sleeping with her. At least, not here. Daniela should have been too tired to speculate. All she wanted to do was lie down and close her eyes for a few minutes.

Taryn paused at the doorway, nibbling at her lower lip. "I thought I should let you know that you don't have to pretend like nothing happened. It must be exhausting, putting on a polite smile for strangers."

Daniela gave her a blank stare.

"Sean told me about the baby," she explained.

The blood drained from her face. "He did?"

"Well, yeah. We've discussed it several times, actually. And I was here the night he got the phone call about the accident. So I knew already."

"You were here," she repeated, her mind going numb. "With him."

"Yes. It was pretty awful, watching him go through that. The Coast Guard wouldn't make a special trip, so he had to wait until the next morning to go back to the mainland. He wanted to take the whaler—alone, with no lights or navigation system, when it was pitch black out." She shook her head, disturbed by the memory. "It was too dangerous, of course, so we couldn't let him. He stayed up all night, pacing the living room, practically going crazy."

Daniela felt her throat tighten. She couldn't imagine Sean acting that way. He was always strong, sensible and calm.

She was the one who panicked, paced rooms and went crazy.

Taryn gave Daniela a closer inspection, frowning at her bewildered expression. "You didn't know?"

"I knew he was here...."

Thankfully, Taryn didn't press for more details. "Anyway, I just wanted to say that I'm sorry for your loss. I know Sean's all torn up about it, too."

"He told you that?"

She blinked her wide blue eyes. "Well, sure. Who wouldn't be?"

Daniela remained silent, unable to answer. Sean hadn't discussed any of his feelings with her. He'd never let her know what he'd gone through that night, never told her how he was dealing with the death of their child. And she'd never asked.

She'd been too busy falling apart.

Daniela wasn't able to comfort Sean in his time of need, or even accept his comfort. After she'd come home from the hospital, she'd been an emotional wreck. Every time he'd tried to reach out to her, she shrank away.

So instead of confiding in her, he'd turned to Taryn. Beautiful, fun-loving, easy-going Taryn.

What man wouldn't be tempted by a knockout blonde?

Taryn glanced around the room. "If you don't need anything else—"

"I just want to be left alone," Daniela said coldly.

Taryn's brow furrowed. She was pretty, but far from dumb. Behind her perfect features and pleasant smile, a not-so-sweet personality lurked. Daniela saw a hard-edged intelligence and a hint of dislike.

"Of course," she said, nodding. Her mouth twisted, making her look even less like a bubbleheaded college student and more like a woman who knew her own mind. Turning, she left the room without another word.

Daniela fell back on the bed the instant she closed the

door. Snubbing Taryn hadn't made her feel any better. She wasn't a vindictive person, and she didn't enjoy hearing about Sean in pain. But she was shocked by the news that he'd opened up to Taryn, after being unable to share his feelings with her.

She hadn't felt this bitter since he'd filed for divorce.

"Damn you," she whispered, punching the pillow beside her. She wasn't sure whom she was angrier with, Sean or herself. She was the one who'd had the emotional breakdown. She was the one who'd driven him away.

She squeezed her eyes shut, bombarded by images of the past and flashes from today. Grinding metal and gnashing teeth.

No one understood, but the least of her worries was personal injury. After spending those agonizing moments trapped in a crushed vehicle, eight months pregnant and literally bleeding to death, she was afraid of confinement and pain.

But her greatest fear, by far, was loss.

Losing their daughter, never experiencing the miracle of her birth, being robbed of her first smiles and first steps and first words…

It was a thousand times more traumatic than any amount of physical distress.

Feeling the agony wash over her, again and again, Daniela curled up in a little ball on the lower bunk, and, pressing her hands to her now-flat stomach, began to cry.

"You want to tell me what's going on?"

Avoiding Jason's question, Sean shoved his hands in his pockets and watched the day fade away, contemplating this crux of his life.

The last rays of sunlight stretched out across the water, hitting the chop and bathing the rippled surface with golden tips. At Skull Rock, only one eye was still visible, glittering darkly, like a demon waiting for the cover of night.

Before Daniela's accident, he'd loved this place.

He'd been fascinated with sharks ever since he was a kid. Point Reyes, his hometown, was just north of San Francisco, in the heart of the Red Triangle. The area encompassed a portion of the California coast, including the Farallon Islands, and boasted more fatal shark attacks on humans than anywhere else in the world.

The summer he turned fifteen, his parents separated, and Sean moved to San Diego with his dad, but he never forget his idyllic childhood in Point Reyes, those halcyon days before the divorce. They'd lived just blocks from the beach, and he and his dad had gone surfing together damn near every day.

One unforgettable morning, when Sean was about twelve, they'd been out on the water, waiting for the next swell. A creepy sensation had come over him, making the hairs on the back of his neck stand up. The "sharky" feeling was one every surfer on the planet recognized. His dad felt it, too. They left the water immediately.

Later that afternoon, another surfer had been bitten by a great white and bled to death on that very beach.

From that moment on, Sean knew what he wanted to do. Studying sharks in general, and the white shark in particular, was his greatest ambition, his ultimate goal, his life's dream. Just being near them made him happy.

Or, it used to.

Now he loathed this island. If he hadn't been trapped here, fulfilling his last professional obligation before he took family leave, he'd have been with Daniela. He'd have been driving instead of her.

"Damn it," he muttered, running a hand through his hair. He wouldn't have agreed to come to the Farallones again if he hadn't owed Dr. Fitzwilliam a favor. Fitz had covered for him during the family emergency.

"Do you think she should stay here?" Jason asked.

"No," he said, his voice grim. The sun had gone below the horizon, taking every hint of warmth with it. "But she says she can handle it."

"What happened to her?"

Sean pulled his gaze from the water. "You don't know?"

"I haven't spent much time in the States for the past couple of years. To be honest, I never connected her name to yours."

He hesitated, reluctant to tell the tragic story. In the weeks following the accident, Sean had been responsible for notifying dozens of friends and family members about Daniela's condition. Although he had the words memorized and could speak them without inflection, they were no easier to say the hundredth time than the first.

"She was in a car accident during the third trimester of her pregnancy," he began, his voice flat. "A drunk driver blindsided her SUV, leaving her trapped inside for several hours. She lost the baby."

Jason stared at him for a moment, trying to process the information. He swallowed hard and put his hand on Sean's shoulder. "Jesus, man. I'm sorry. Really sorry. That's terrible."

Sean clenched his jaw, hating this part of the process. But then, he hated all the parts. He knew Jason meant well, but Sean felt like a bear with a thorn in his paw. Watching another man comfort his wife, when he couldn't, had put him in a very dark mood.

It was all he could do not to shrug off Jason's touch. He was more interested in a rousing fistfight than this clumsy display of kindness.

"I had no idea," Jason continued, a pained expression on his face. "No wonder she's having a hard time."

"Yeah, well, maybe you should have done a basic background check before you signed her on." He cast Jason a cutting glance. "Although, judging by the look of the crew this season, I can guess the criteria you used to make your selections."

Jason dropped his hand. "What's that supposed to mean?"

Knowing he was being an asshole, and not giving a damn, Sean tilted his chin toward the house. "All of the ladies inside are very easy on the eyes. I don't think you could find a prettier group of female scientists if you tried."

The jibe was beneath them both. And Sean couldn't have cared less.

To his credit, Jason refused to take him seriously. "I chose them based on expertise and project diversity, not physical appearance, but what can I say? I got lucky. Next time you visit, I'll make sure the girls are uglier."

Sean shook his head and sighed, his anger fading as quickly as it came. Jason was impossible to stay mad at. And Sean couldn't begrudge his appreciation for the opposite sex; he'd always liked the ladies, himself. Although his parents' divorce had been bitter, and his own more devastating still, he continued to enjoy the company of women.

Just not with the same…vigor.

Daniela used to tease him about his female friends, calling them his "followers," but she'd never acted jealous. Not even when he was working in the field for weeks at a time. Of course, he'd always jumped on her the instant he walked through the door. It was one of the aspects of their relationship he missed most. He'd loved coming home to her after spending time apart. They'd never been able to get enough of each other.

"Let's keep a close eye on her for the next few days," Jason said, returning to the topic of most importance. "She can always go back to the mainland if she needs to. The last thing I want is for anyone to get hurt here."

Feeling his throat tighten, Sean moved his gaze to the uneven shoreline, watching midnight-blue water slosh and slap against gray, perforated rocks. In the distance, the Skull was shrouded in darkness now, wearing an impenetrable mask.

Chapter 4

As Daniela came down the stairs, the aroma of sautéed vegetables and the sizzle of oil assailed her senses, along with the faint, sweet fragrance of sticky rice.

She was hungry, she realized with surprise. Really hungry.

Jason was in the kitchen, doing his magic. The top half of his black hair, which was even longer than Sean's, was caught up in a Samurai ponytail. Despite the chill, his upper body was clad in a thin white T-shirt. The muscles in his arms flexed as he moved the sauté pan, and the edge of a tattoo flashed from beneath one short sleeve.

He was very nice to look at, but her eyes slipped by him almost immediately, resting instead on Sean. Her ex-husband stood in the back of the kitchen, leaning against the counter with a beer bottle in his hand.

Men. Hot water wasn't a necessity, but they always had beer.

Under the harsh fluorescent light, he appeared older than the last time she'd seen him, a little wearier and a lot more weathered. His hair was still the same thick golden-brown, his eyes the same shade of dark honey and his skin as tanned as ever, but his demeanor had changed. When his gaze met hers, it was shuttered. He was hiding something from her, and he'd never done that before.

Daniela became aware that a hush had fallen over the room. On the other side of a wall partition, but in full view of the kitchen, Taryn and Elizabeth were seated at the dinner table, laptops open. After a brief pause, they resumed tapping at the keys.

Brent Masterson stood by the front window, hands in his pants pockets, as still and quiet as a shadow. He gave her a wry smile, acknowledging the awkward moment rather than pretending it wasn't there.

She drew in a deep, calming breath. "What can I do to help?"

"You can set the table," Jason said. He pointed with the spatula, indicating the cabinet behind Sean. "Plates are up there."

The kitchen was small, and she had to get very close to Sean in order to take the plates down. He flattened his back against the side of the refrigerator, but her elbow still almost touched his chest as she opened the cabinet door. The dark green sweater he was wearing looked familiar—she'd given it to him for Christmas, at least five years ago. Like him, it appeared a little worse for the wear. Used hard and work-roughened.

Not that it mattered, on his body. Even threadbare, wash-faded fabric suited his rangy, well-muscled frame.

Swallowing drily, she looked up into the cabinet. A stack of colorful ceramic plates sat on the top shelf.

"Do you need me to get them?" he asked.

"I can reach," she said, standing on tiptoe. He was so close she could feel the heat of his body and smell his skin. If she lived to be a hundred years old, she would never forget his scent, warm and musky and deliciously masculine.

Sean.

She took down the stack of sturdy, mismatched plates, aware of his proximity and his watchful eyes.

Her red long-sleeved thermal was a utilitarian item, sturdy and comfortable, but it fit snugly, outlining her breasts. She'd always had trouble finding clothes that weren't too tight across the chest. Under Sean's gaze, the fabric seemed to shrink further, making her feel overwarm and underdressed.

It wasn't as if he was ogling her. It was just that she couldn't help but think of the many times he'd lifted her against any convenient flat surface, including the kitchen countertops, in their apartment.

Heat rose to her cheeks. The memories seemed foreign to her, as if those intimacies belonged to someone else. The person she'd become didn't respond like that, tearing a man's clothes off as soon as he walked through the door.

The woman she was now didn't respond at all.

"Silverware?" she murmured, avoiding eye contact.

"In the top drawer," Jason said. "Just forks will do."

Nodding, she counted out six forks and placed them on top of the stack. Adding a handful of napkins, she carried the bundle to the table, trying not to let her arm brush against Sean's midsection as she walked out of the kitchen.

Elizabeth and Taryn put their laptops away, helping Daniela set the table.

After Jason brought out the food, there was a minor commotion as everyone gathered around the table. When

Sean took the seat opposite Daniela, she found herself staring at him. She dropped her gaze to the forest-green knit across his chest, her heart racing in a way that had nothing to do with anxiety.

The sweater was seven years old, now that she thought about it. She'd given it to him on Christmas Eve, the same night he'd proposed. He'd hidden the ring in a lingerie box with a ridiculously sexy red teddy.

It was a joke, because he knew she hated gifts like that. She hadn't seen the ring at first. Annoyed by his poor taste, giving her trashy underwear on Christmas, after she'd bought him an expensive sweater, she'd almost thrown the box at him.

Then she saw his eyes sparkle with humor, and she looked again, finding the diamond. With a smile, he got down on one knee and asked her to be his wife.

That night, she'd worn the ring *and* the teddy.

Daniela rubbed the empty place on her finger, blinking away the memories. Now the ring was hiding in a jewelry box at the back of her lingerie drawer. The teddy was in shreds, having been torn from her body by Sean on one of his homecomings. Blushing slightly, she lifted her gaze from the sweater to his shadowed jaw.

His scruffy, don't-give-a-damn appearance only added to his appeal.

In contrast, Brent, to his right, seemed almost elegant. And then there was Jason. With his dark good looks and easy smile, he had an edgy style that was neither rugged nor refined.

All three men were handsome—and eligible—as far as Daniela knew. The table seemed to shrink in their presence, and she felt acutely self-conscious. She couldn't remember the last time she'd eaten a meal with strangers.

Jason proposed a toast. "To new beginnings?"

"To new beginnings," Brent agreed, lifting his own glass.

Sean's expression was sardonic, but he went along with it, and Daniela followed suit, clinking her water bottle against Taryn's. It didn't escape her attention that a barren, inhospitable island was an ironic choice as a place to start over.

Jason served the *lumpia* fresh, rather than fried, and it was a build-your-own affair. The ingredients were placed in the center of the table, and everything looked delicious.

Daniela scooped up sautéed vegetables and shredded chicken, the filling for the moist, paper-thin wrappers. Rolling them up into neat little packages wasn't easy, and no one but Jason was entirely successful. Although she was hungry, her frayed nerves wreaked havoc on her appetite, so she focused on chewing and swallowing, one small bite at a time.

"This is your first visit to the Farallones, Daniela?" Brent asked.

"Yes," she said, glancing up from her plate. "How about you?"

"It's my first time, too. And Elizabeth's, I think?"

She nodded.

"That can't have been the first time you'd seen a shark attack," Daniela commented. "You were as cool as ice."

Laughing, he shook his head. "I was scared witless, I assure you. But you're right, I've filmed sharks feeding many times. The trick is to cultivate a courageous facade." Arching a brow at Sean, he asked, "Or do you become inured to it, eventually?"

Sean shrugged. "It would be a mistake to get too comfortable out there."

"Says the man whose pulse never climbs above seventy."

Sean lifted a forkful of rice to his mouth, not bothering to dispute him.

"Well, you couldn't pay me to watch a shark feeding," Elizabeth said with a shudder. "If this island wasn't home to so many species of birds, I wouldn't have come at all."

Brent gave her an odd look. "Really? I could have sworn I'd met you before, on a shark expedition. I've been wracking my brain, trying to remember where and when."

Jason perked up at this news. "Liz is secretly a shark groupie?"

"Don't be absurd," she said, her tone frosty. "I hate sharks."

"My mistake," Brent murmured, but Daniela was left with the impression that he didn't think it was.

The tension in the room was palpable. Elizabeth seemed uneasy in her surroundings, and reluctant to share personal information. Sean wasn't thrilled with Daniela's unexpected arrival. And Taryn picked at her food, looking depressed by the turn of events.

"I heard that the house is haunted," Daniela said, changing the subject.

Unfortunately, her attempt to lighten the mood failed. No one said a word.

"Is there a local superstition?" she asked, pressing on.

Taryn stopped pretending to eat and set her fork down. Sean shot her a warning glare but she ignored it. "Some people think the house is inhabited by a lady in white. She was a light keeper's wife, a pioneer woman who lived here a hundred years ago."

"What's her story?"

Her lips curved into a humorless smile. "Apparently, she threw herself off the cliffs. One night, she went to the lighthouse tower to check the lamps. Instead of refueling them, she walked to the edge and leaped to her death."

A chill traveled down Daniela's spine. "How do they know she jumped?"

"She washed up at Dead Man's Beach, pockets full of stones."

"Oh." Now she knew why Sean hadn't wanted her to hear the tale. He'd always been protective, and there was a time, not so long ago, that she'd contemplated a similar fate. "Why wasn't she eaten by sharks, do you think?"

"It wasn't shark season," Jason said, matter-of-fact.

Daniela stared down at her plate, silent. She was curious about the skinned seal, but she hesitated to bring up a second unpleasant topic. Instead, she ate a few more bites and took sips of water, pretending to relax.

After the dinner plates were cleared, Sean disappeared into the office, Brent cleaned his camera equipment and Jason washed dishes.

Taryn and Elizabeth took out their laptops to write daily logs.

Daniela hadn't brought hers, as she preferred to write notes by hand and input the information later. There was another computer in the office, an older desk model that stayed on the island, but Sean was using it.

She wandered over to the bookcase, perusing its contents. There were a lot of dog-eared paperbacks, mostly fantasy and science fiction. Not what she was looking for. "Have you always done computerized logs?"

"No," Taryn said. "There's a stack of ledgers in the cabinet."

"Ah." The wooden cabinet was situated against the back wall, above an old Formica countertop. Daniela opened the cabinet doors, eying the rows of books with interest. Being vertically challenged, she couldn't reach the back, or see all the way inside.

"I'll get them," Elizabeth offered.

"That's okay," she muttered, boosting herself up and perching one hip on the edge of the countertop. "Short girls know how to get by."

In addition to the ledgers, she found dozens of history books, some decades old. She took them out, one by one, smoothing her hands over the scarred leather surfaces. There would be a wealth of information here.

The story about the lady in white had piqued her interest. Since her own near-death experience, she had a morbid fascination with other people's tragedies.

After choosing one of the newest ledgers, and the most intriguing history text, she put the other books back in the cabinet. Taking a seat in the armchair in the far corner, because it couldn't be seen from the office, she opened the ledger. Sean's jagged scrawl leaped out at her from the pages, line after line of dark, confident script.

When they were married, he'd often written her notes in the morning before he left the house. Nothing wildly romantic, because that wasn't his style. Just your basic grocery lists and gentle reminders and the occasional "I love you."

Putting those notes out of her mind, with some difficulty, she flipped though the pages of the ledger. A single date jumped out at her: September 25th, just over two years ago. The anniversary of the accident.

Sean had jotted down the time and a detailed description of an incident with the cage-diving crew. Apparently, he'd driven the whaler out to their diving boat to ask them to stop chumming, and some four-letter words had been exchanged. Just as the dialogue started getting interesting, the script cut off, midsentence. There were no new entries from Sean until recently. He must have been writing this when he heard—

Daniela closed the book abruptly. She picked up the history text instead, learning about the islands' tumultuous past.

When the words began to blur on the page, she knew it was time to turn in. She'd taken a red-eye flight from San Diego to San Francisco, and a rocky, four-hour boat trip from there out to the islands. Her afternoon had been spent watching a shark attack. She'd had a difficult day, to say the least.

Although it was still early, just shy of 9:00 p.m., she was dead tired.

"I'm beat," Taryn said, echoing her thoughts. "I won't be able to drag myself out of bed at the crack of dawn if I stay up much longer."

Murmuring in agreement, everyone else began to put their work materials away. Daniela returned the books to the cabinet, and Elizabeth ducked into the downstairs bathroom.

Brent, who'd just gone outside, came back in, bringing a rush of cold night air and the faint scent of tobacco with him. It wasn't the acrid stench of filtered cigarettes, but the mild aroma of roll-your-owns. The smell reminded Daniela of her father.

"I guess I'm ready to go upstairs," she said to Taryn.

The girl forced a smile. "Good night, then," she said, nodding at the others.

"Good night," Daniela parroted, avoiding Sean, who had come out of the office. It hurt too much to remember all the nights they'd spent together, most of which had been very good indeed.

In their shared room, Taryn kicked off her furry boots and climbed into the top bunk, her body a slight curve beneath her sleeping bag. Daniela changed quickly, removing her weatherproof trousers and pulling on soft flannel pajama pants. After laying her own sleeping bag on the lower bunk, she slipped inside, reaching out to turn off the lamp.

She froze, thinking about frigid air and black nothingness. Gushing blood and razor-sharp teeth.

"There's a night-light," Taryn said, her voice muffled by blankets.

"What?"

"There's a night-light. It turns on automatically."

"You're afraid of the dark?" she asked.

The question was met by silence. After a pause, Taryn said, "No. But this house is really creepy. Sometimes I wake up and feel out of breath. The dark can be suffocating."

Daniela's antagonism toward the girl softened. "My panic attacks are like that," she admitted. "I know what you mean."

"If you can't sleep with it on, I'll unplug it."

"No," she said, switching off the lamp. The night-light in the corner illuminated a small section of the wall, creating a halo effect. Chasing the shadows away. "It's fine. Waking up in a strange place can be disorienting, and…I have nightmares."

"If I hear you, should I wake you up?"

She rolled onto her back and closed her eyes, struck by a slew of unpleasant memories. Not all of her nights with Sean had been good. Sometimes, she'd woken up screaming, hitting him with both fists.

"No," she said, hugging her arms around her waist. "Don't wake me."

Daniela opened her eyes with a start, her heart pounding against her ribs, her breath coming in quick, short pants. In the bunk above her, Taryn's sleeping form caused an almost imperceptible dip in the thin mattress.

No hint of light peeked through the window. The desk clock read 1:45 a.m.

Fumbling for the bottled water at her bedside, she took a slow sip, struggling to regulate her breathing and hold her panic at bay.

Her nightmares came less frequently now, but they still came. She'd figured sleep would be elusive in these strange surroundings. To her surprise, exhaustion had overtaken her and she'd drifted off, minutes after lying down.

She'd dreamed of being trapped inside the 4Runner, impaled on a piece of twisted metal frame. Intermittent rain came through the broken front windshield, wetting her cheeks, rousing her from semiconsciousness. With lucidity came pain and terror and sorrow. She turned her face away, seeking to drown herself in the bliss of sleep.

Sean's hand reached out, yanking her from the car. Pulling her out of comfort's arms and away from sweet oblivion.

The nightmare was always the same.

When her heart no longer threatened to burst from her chest, she rose from the lower bunk, her sock-covered feet padding silently across the hardwood floor. Outside of her cozy sleeping bag, the air was bracingly cold.

Shivering, she eased into her hooded sweatshirt and slipped out the door. When she had bad dreams, she preferred to get up and move around. She knew from experience that going right back to sleep was impossible, and lying in bed only increased her anxiety.

Pacing the hallway was out, so she went downstairs to make a cup of tea. Walking was therapeutic, but simple tasks also calmed her nerves.

Halfway down the stairs, she felt a chill. In fact, she could *see* it. Fog crept up the stairwell, curling around her fuzzy wool socks.

The front door was open.

Daniela couldn't believe her eyes. Had someone just left the house, in the dead of night? Even more unsettling, had an unexpected visitor dropped in?

For a moment, fear kept her rooted to the spot. She imagined diaphanous white gowns and dead limbs, rising from the mist.

"Don't be a fool," she whispered, shaking her head. Perhaps she was prone to panic attacks and crying jags, but she wasn't fanciful or weak-minded.

Straightening her shoulders, she hurried down the last few steps, moving toward the front door with purpose. The wind had forced it open, nothing more. Brent hadn't closed it properly during his last smoke break.

She took a quick peek outside, making sure he wasn't standing there now, puffing away. She didn't see anything but fog, so she drew it closed, shutting out the cold air and silencing the sound of the crashing surf.

When a hand touched her shoulder, she almost jumped out of her skin.

It was Jason.

"Puta madre!" she gasped, her heart in her throat.

He chuckled at her colorful language, his teeth very white in the dark. "I'm sorry. I thought you were sleep-walking."

"You scared the hell out of me."

"I can see that," he said, still smiling.

"Were you going out for a stroll?" he asked.

"Of course not. The door was open when I came downstairs."

His expression sobered. "Are you serious?"

"Dead serious."

Frowning, he opened the door again, doing a quick search of the foggy exterior before he shrugged and closed it. After a moment's deliberation, he engaged the dead bolt.

"You don't usually lock it?" Daniela asked him.

"No reason to."

She followed his logic. The island had no docking facilities, so it wasn't as though any vandals or rabble-rousers could drop by. "Must have been the wind," she murmured, wrapping her arms around her body.

He looked past her, studying the dark living room for signs of a disturbance. Everything was in its place.

"Sean told me about the skinned seal," she said.

His brows rose in surprise. "Are you worried about that? I'm sure it was an isolated incident."

She shrugged, crossing her arms over her chest. "I had a bad dream," she said. "I came downstairs to make a cup of tea."

His eyes softened with sympathy. "Would you like some company?"

Over the past two years, she'd been asked that question many times. With very few exceptions, she'd said no. She hadn't wanted company of any kind. Everyone, including Sean, had been desperate to console her. But she'd been inconsolable.

Hiding herself away, locked in misery, was easier than interacting with people, and she'd needed time to be alone with her grief.

At long last, that phase had passed.

"Yes," she said, taking a deep breath. "I would like company. Very much."

Chapter 5

When Daniela awoke again, the room was gray with pre-dawn light. She was surprised she'd slept so well. After a quiet conversation with Jason, and a hot cup of tea, she'd returned to bed, but she hadn't expected a restful night.

Taryn was still in the upper bunk, her breathing soft and even.

Daniela slipped out of bed, shivering. It was chillier than it had been a few hours ago. Moving quickly, she grabbed her toiletries kit instead of her work clothes. It would be easier to get dressed after she went to the bathroom.

Still groggy from sleep, she didn't realize someone was already using the facilities until she was standing outside the door. The sound of running water stopped abruptly, and before she had a chance to retreat, the door opened.

Sean stepped into the hallway, a towel wrapped around his waist, his gloriously bare chest mere inches from her face.

They both froze.

She'd seen him more naked than this hundreds of times, from every possible angle, and he'd never shown a hint of modesty. Nor an ounce of shame. But, to be fair, what shame was there in having a body that could make a grown woman weep?

He was leaner than he'd been a few years ago, and even more toned, every muscle in his body standing out in clear definition. He looked like a human anatomy chart.

Although a part of her suspected his exercise regimen had been a little *too* grueling lately, she couldn't help but stare at the hard planes of his chest and the straits along his rib cage. Her eyes followed the furrow of dark hair on his abdomen until it disappeared under the damp towel, which was slung precariously low on his hips.

She forced her gaze up to his face.

His expression was guarded, awaiting her reaction. He smelled fantastic, like clean water and spicy soap. Her mouth watered at the tantalizing scent, and her fingertips itched to touch his skin, but her mind registered that there was something out of place. Although she could swear she felt heat coming off his body, there was no shower steam.

"No hot water?" she blurted.

A flush stole across his cheekbones. "Not much."

Because she was standing there like a moron, blocking his exit, he went around her, gripping his towel in a clenched fist.

Entranced, she watched him go. When he switched hands on the towel to turn the doorknob to his bedroom, the terry cloth slipped down another inch, rewarding her with a glimpse of his tautly defined hip.

As soon as he was out of sight, she snapped out of her

stupor. What was wrong with her? He must think her an utter fool.

Smothering a moan of embarrassment, she stumbled forward into the tiny bathroom and pulled the door shut behind her. The woman in the mirror above the sink stared back at her in dismay, her skin too pale for her almost-black hair, eyes too big for her face.

Her nostrils flared, inhaling his soap, his skin, his scent.

Even his dirty clothes, which he'd left in a mesh bag on the tile floor, smelled better than a field of wildflowers to her sadly man-deprived nose. Fisting her hands in her hair, she sank into a crouched position, letting her back slide down the door.

She hadn't realized how much she'd missed him.

When they were together, there was nothing he wouldn't do to please her. In the months following the accident, he'd wanted to comfort her more than ever. Instead of taking advantage of that opportunity, she'd shied away from his touch.

In hindsight, she should have expected him to file for divorce. His need for physical intimacy had never waned, not once over the course of their five-year marriage, not even during her pregnancy. If anything, he'd reached for her more often, fascinated by the changes in her body, exploring every new curve.

After losing the baby, she'd had no interest in sex, and he hadn't pressed the issue at first. When he had…it was the beginning of the end.

At the time of their separation, they hadn't been intimate in over a year.

Sean had never been a monk. He was a man of strong appetites, and there would always be women lining up to indulge him. She didn't think he'd cheated. But how often had he been in a remote location with a sweet young thing like Taryn? And how could she assume he would go without female attention while he was away if he wasn't getting any at home?

Angry with herself for wondering—and for caring—she lurched to her feet. It hardly mattered if Sean had been faithful during their marriage.

It was over. Time to move on.

To say she had regrets was an understatement, but she'd come here to start again, not to dwell on the past, or to re-immerse herself in a pit of despair.

With swift, impatient motions, she turned on the faucet and bent over the sink. Cupping her hands together, she filled them with ice-cold water, gritting her teeth as she washed the dazed look off her face.

Cursing his unruly body for having a predictable reaction to the sight of his beautiful ex-wife, who looked enticingly sleep-rumpled and adorably mussed, Sean rifled through his belongings, searching for his deodorant.

"Damn," he muttered, realizing he'd left his dirty laundry in the bathroom. He wasn't going back for it until she'd cleared out of there.

Taking the cap off his deodorant, he swiped it under his arms and tossed the stick back into his pack. He'd stripped out of his wetsuit on a public beach more times than he could count, so towel-changing was second nature to him. Employing the same technique, he kept the terry cloth wrapped around his waist while he pulled on his boxer briefs, moving quickly because it was damned cold.

He'd tossed and turned most of the night, trying not to think about the way Daniela's red thermal shirt cupped her luscious breasts. He wished he couldn't imagine, in agonizing detail, the silkiness of her skin beneath his fingertips, the sounds she made when she climaxed and the soft cushion of her body under his.

She made him feel like an ungainly adolescent, with no control over his reactions. Christ, they'd been together for almost ten years. He should be bored by the sight of her in comfy pajamas, not reduced to drooling.

If nothing else, the cold shower should have kept him in check. He hadn't expected to respond to her proximity, but when her eyes drifted down his belly, he'd felt a powerful jolt of lust, and could only hope she hadn't noticed.

One almost-glance from a woman he longed to forget had him swelling with arousal, remembering far too much.

"Damn it," he said under his breath, kicking into his pants. It wasn't his fault she was still wearing that snug-fitting red top. And those baggy flannel pajama bottoms wouldn't have been sexy if he didn't know how easy it was to slip his hand inside the elastic waistband. One tug, and they would slide down her curvy hips.

Jason roused, throwing back his sleeping bag. He frowned at Sean blearily. "It was my turn to shower."

"Be my guest. I didn't use any hot water."

His drowsy eyes narrowed. "You took a cold shower on purpose? What the hell is wrong with you?"

Scowling, Sean draped his towel over a chair and pulled on his jeans. Before he was finished buttoning his fly, Daniela appeared in the doorway, holding his mesh laundry bag. Her gaze wandered down his bare torso, coming to an abrupt halt at his fumbling hands.

"Oh," Jason said. "Now I get it."

Dani blinked at him, curious. "Get what?"

"Never mind," Sean said, leaving his top button undone. Stepping forward, he took the laundry bag from her. "Thanks."

"No problem," she said, retreating into the hallway.

Jason gave Sean a knowing smirk. "Does she rattle your cage?"

"Shut up," he muttered, lobbing the laundry bag at his bunk. To his disappointment, it missed Jason by a mile.

"She's a beautiful woman."

Sean couldn't stop himself from growling, "Stay away from her."

Jason laughed, letting his head fall back against the pillows. "I've never seen you act so stupid. I'm relieved by the evidence that you might actually be human. I was beginning to think you were a robot."

Although Jason's words annoyed him, they also spurred him into action. Moving quickly, he tugging on a sweatshirt and went after Daniela. "Hang on a sec," he said, catching her before she entered her room.

She turned to face him, her expression wary.

A few damp strands of hair clung to her slender throat, and her breath smelled minty-fresh. He'd always liked kissing her before she brushed just as well as after, but right now he was struck by the powerful urge to press her back to the wall and taste every inch of her delicious mouth.

He massaged his forehead, wishing he could scrub the temptation away. *Focus, Sean.* "How are you?" he asked inanely.

Her brow furrowed. "I'm fine."

"No...nightmares?"

"I'm fine," she repeated, crossing her arms over her chest.

"Because I thought we could..." He faltered, floundering like a teenager asking her out for their first date. "We usually give newcomers an island tour. Taryn and Elizabeth will show you around the lighthouse, and take you out to the blinds, where they do research, but the best way to see the Steller is by boat."

Her eyes brightened with interest. At certain times, she was so beautiful it pained him to look at her. "Will Jason go?" she asked, her excitement at viewing wildlife in their natural habitat tempered only by her distaste for being alone in his company.

"Yeah, sure," he said, forcing a smile.

She smiled back at him. "Okay, then. That would be great. Thanks."

"Great," he muttered, raking a hand through his hair. Just great.

As soon as she disappeared into the room she shared with Taryn, he went down the hall, his jaw clenched. What was he thinking? He wasn't the welcoming committee. He didn't even want Daniela to stay here.

Not just for her own good. For his.

He hadn't mentioned this to Jason, but her panic attacks could be extremely debilitating. After the accident, he'd watched her withdraw from reality on numerous occasions, almost to the point of becoming unresponsive.

Her nightmares were no less troubling. She'd bloodied his nose during one of the worst episodes. He'd gripped her wrists tightly, trying to calm her down, and she'd gone ballistic, screaming for him to let her go. From then on, he'd taken the hits without complaint. In a sad, dysfunctional way, her glancing blows were better than nothing.

It was the only time she touched him.

Pushing aside the memories, which were best left in the past—like his relationship with Daniela—he put on his boots, ignoring Jason's amused expression. Downstairs, Elizabeth was sitting at the table, drinking coffee and reading, a pair of stretchy black gloves covering her slender hands.

"Morning," she murmured, not bothering to glance up.

"Good morning," he replied, ducking into the kitchen.

Still unsettled by the chance encounter with Dani, he located his portable mug in the kitchen cabinet and filled it to the brim with hot coffee. His knee-jerk sexual response to her was a simple matter of compatible physical chemistry.

Hard to predict, impossible to control.

It didn't mean he was doomed to pine for her forever. He just needed to rewire his system. Reprogram his thinking. Engage with other women.

Other women. Like Elizabeth.

On his way out the door, he paused, studying the pretty redhead in a new light. Although he found her attractive, Sean had never been curious about her sexually. He stared at her for a moment now, trying to drum up some interest. She wasn't built like Daniela, but neither was she skinny. He appreciated curves on women, and he could see that she had her share.

She had a nice figure. He just wasn't eager to explore it. The idea of sleeping with her didn't tempt him half as much as the faint scent of Daniela's toothpaste.

"What's wrong?" she asked, noticing his perusal. She smoothed her hand down the front of her sweater, as if checking for crumbs.

"Nothing," he said, dragging his mind out of the gutter. "What are you up to today?"

"I'm going to the bird blind to collect waste samples. That's why I'm dressed in these old rags." She smiled ruefully. "Ready to get bombarded."

"Oh." Smiling back at her, he took a sip of coffee. Before now, he'd thought she was a little too reserved. After one harmless confession, she seemed much more down to earth.

Or maybe imagining her naked had done the trick. "You look fine to me."

She tucked a strand of hair behind her ear. "Thanks."

"Where are you from?"

"Florida, originally. Daytona Beach."

"Shark central."

Her eyes darkened. "Yes. There are more incidental attacks there than anywhere else in the world. More people in the water."

Sean warmed up to the subject. "Ever had a run-in?"

"No. I don't swim."

"You're joking."

She shook her head.

"Well, you have to learn. What if you fell off a boat, or—"

"Around here? Drowning would be the least of my worries." As if the conversation were finished, she opened her book and resumed reading. *Water Birds of the Pacific Coast,* ironically enough.

It took him a second to realize he'd been snubbed. Elizabeth was a cool customer, and Sean had been amused by Jason's attempts to woo her over the past few days. She'd shot him down a number of times.

Sean hadn't expected to get the same treatment.

He ducked his head, smothering a self-deprecating laugh. If he wanted to talk to a woman, he could at least find a willing one—like Taryn. "I'm on shark watch," he said, muttering goodbye as he headed out the door.

The hike up to the tower was daunting.

A zigzagged path dealt with the sharp rise in elevation, and traversing it was akin to walking up a thousand stairs. The most dangerous area, a narrow space at the outer edge of the cliff, had a sturdy wooden handrail for additional support. A sheer drop on that side careened down the cliff at almost fifty feet, ending at a section of water they called the Washtub. Incoming waves converged there in a swirl of powerful currents.

The safety rail didn't calm Daniela's nerves. She could easily imagine flipping over it, falling into the treacherous waters below.

Once they reached the summit, and she had her feet planted on stable ground, she breathed a sigh of relief. Her chest was heaving and her leg muscles burned from exertion, but these were pleasant aches.

Perspiration covered her face like a fine sea mist.

The lighthouse tower afforded a three hundred and sixty degree view of the island, which made it an ideal location for shark watch. Sean was standing there now, binoculars poised. The tower itself was empty, its upper floors barred to keep out wild animals. Near the edge of the cliff, an unsightly metal structure housed the automated beacon. A flashing blip had replaced the bright lamps of the past, and the high-powered Fresnel lens had long since been retired to the mainland.

The scientists' duties didn't include guiding passing ships in the night.

Before the U.S. Coast Guard took over, a light keeper had kept the lamps going by hand. In the past, hundreds of people had stayed on Southeast Farallon, but few had considered it home. Early hunters had visited seasonally, sleeping in sealskin tents. Egg collectors, who raided murre nests for a meager wage during a time when chickens were scarce in San Francisco, rarely battled the elements to attempt permanent lodgings.

After the lighthouse was constructed, entire families had lived here. It was a hard life for men, even more so for women and children. The only fresh water came from a trickling ravine, dripping down over the face of the cliff like sweat from a wrung-out towel. When the weather was bad, no supplies could be brought in, and food was scarce.

With unreliable access to medical care, many sick children died of curable illnesses.

Daniela had learned all of this last night in the history book, which had offered an unflinching depiction of the island's quality of life. The author of the text hadn't romanticized the harsh conditions in any way.

And yet, standing atop the lighthouse hill, with the enormity of the Pacific Ocean around her and the immensity of the blue sky above, she was…exhilarated. Yes, this place was intimidating, even scary, but there was a strange, stark beauty here, too.

It was sort of like climbing Mount Everest. Few people had earned this opportunity. She felt as though she was on top of the world.

Taryn's expression was proud. "Beautiful, isn't it?"

"Yes," Daniela admitted, looking out at the dark blue horizon. It was a cold day, brisk and invigorating, a pleasant mix of clouds and sun. Early fall was her favorite time of year.

Or, it used to be.

"Sea Lion Cove is just there," Taryn said, pointing down the opposite side of the hill. "There are a number of convenient haul-outs."

Daniela could see dozens of tawny bodies, fat and supine, basking on the flat rocks along the shore. Much of the island's perimeter was sheer cliff, and they weren't the most graceful climbers. They needed haul-outs for easy access to and from the water.

"And that's Dead Man's Beach."

Next to the cove, there were more sea lions, sunbathing

on an inviting stretch of pale yellow sand. The small beach was edged by steep rock on three sides, which probably made it hard to get to, except via watercraft. During high tide, any boat stranded there would be dashed against the rocks by pounding surf.

Hence, the name.

Daniela pictured the light keeper's wife, lying wet and motionless on the sand, her white skirts tangled around her legs, face gray. As she blinked that disturbing image away, another came to mind. "Where was the skinned pup found?"

"On the north side," Elizabeth answered, gesturing in the general direction. "Jason has been doing some routine checks of the area, but we're supposed to avoid it."

"The boogeyman lives there," Taryn said, rolling her eyes.

"It's well off the beaten path, anyway," Elizabeth said.

Daniela nodded, wondering what kind of sick person would kill a baby seal. Skinning had been illegal in this country for years, and this was an incredibly inconvenient place to commit a crime. Who could have done it, and where had they gone? Even if the island had a secret stowaway, no one could survive here without shelter.

She moved her eyes beyond the shore, staring out at the endless sea. A few hundred yards from the beach, there was a nice-looking break, creating a curling barrel of water that stretched far and wide.

"The Perfect Wave," Taryn said with reverence.

"Jason wants to ride it," Elizabeth added.

"No," Daniela breathed, dragging her gaze away from the shoreline. "You must be joking."

Elizabeth arched a brow at Sean, who was standing near them. Every day during shark season, one of the researchers kept an eye on the water. He'd been there since sunup. "Who do you think gave him the idea?"

He took the binoculars away from his eyes. "He won't do it."

Daniela's stomach clenched at the thought of anyone paddling out into these waters. "You two have discussed this?"

"Yeah, we've discussed it," he said, growing defensive. "Every surfer who's seen that wave has talked about riding it. That's all it is. Big talk."

The women exchanged a glance, conveying a silent message about male stupidity.

"I surf," Taryn pointed out, "and I've never once considered getting in the water here. It's suicide."

Elizabeth and Daniela turned to stare at Sean.

"What are you looking at me for? I wouldn't go out there, either. Jason is the maniac who wants to do it."

"You haven't discouraged him," Elizabeth said quietly.

His eyes darkened. "He isn't serious."

"And if he is?"

"Then you can discourage him," he said, putting the binoculars back up to his face. "You're good at it."

Daniela sucked in a sharp breath, stifling the urge to apologize for Sean's rudeness. He wasn't usually so brusque with women. His handsome face and friendly demeanor had attracted a legion of adoring females.

She hadn't thought him capable of being standoffish.

Taryn shot him a dirty look. "You're grouchy this morning. Did you get up on the wrong side of the bed, or what?"

He let the binoculars drop a few inches, glancing at Daniela, then quickly away. "Jason couldn't surf that wave without help. Someone would have to take him out there in the whaler, and I would never do it." His gaze met Elizabeth's. "Is that better?"

"Much," she said, but her smile was chilly.

Well. There was no love lost between these two.

Taryn wrinkled her nose and moved on. "The bird-watching blind is closer, so we'll go there first," she said, gesturing toward a small outbuilding on the west side of the island. "Elizabeth can tell us all about the research she's been doing."

While the Farallones were famous for the great white sharks that came to feed on the plentiful seals and sea lions, one glance across the rocky isles proved they were first and foremost a habitat for birds.

On Southeast Farallon alone, there were more than half a million. The flat haul-outs near the shore were ideal for lounging sea lions, but the rest of the jagged terrain was bird territory. Every inch of space, every dip and peak, every nook and cranny, housed a roost.

There were cormorants and auklets, storm petrels and pelicans. Rare breeds, like the black-footed albatross and tufted puffin, could be spotted in the same general area as the common murre and Western Gull.

As they hiked toward the blind, hoods of their jackets pulled up to protect them from the inevitable outcome of having so many winged creatures overhead, the cacophony was deafening. Hundreds of thousands of birds, cawing, screeching, twittering, individual voices blending together in a chaotic blur of sound.

It was pure lunacy.

Daniela followed Taryn into the outbuilding, overcome with relief when Elizabeth pulled the door shut behind her, muting the noise.

"Can you believe it's not even breeding season?"

Daniela's ears were ringing, her senses reeling. "You mean this gets worse?"

"God, yes," Taryn said. "The gulls are brutal in spring. They'll dive-bomb anything. Last year Jason was out here, walking around in the open, and one of them almost knocked him unconscious. They're crazy."

Elizabeth bristled. "They do what they need to do to survive, just like any other animal. I don't hear anyone calling sharks crazy."

"True, but some species of birds are vicious. They eat their own young, rob other nests, swoop down with so much striking power that they actually kill themselves during an attack." Taryn shrugged. "You have to admit, that is odd behavior."

Daniela didn't say so, but she agreed with Taryn. Flying scavengers weren't her favorite. "What's your area of interest?"

"Dolphins," she said simply. "I love them."

Of course she did, Daniela thought wryly. All young, idealistic surfer girls who wanted to save the world loved dolphins.

While Elizabeth outlined the basic premise of her research project, which had to do with the harmful effects of chemical pollutants on coastal birds, Daniela peered through the slotted peephole that gave the blind its name.

At eye level, there were several narrow openings in the wall of the outbuilding, allowing scientists to observe wildlife without being seen.

On the westernmost edge of the island, a flock of cormorants glided through the air, making a lazy tornado above an object hidden between two rocks near the shore.

Their shiny black feathers glinted in the sun, catching the reflection off the water.

"Something's dying out there," Taryn murmured, watching them circle.

Chapter 6

At midmorning, Sean lowered his binoculars, watching Jason hike up the hill. Brent followed close behind, carrying his video equipment.

He felt a twinge of trepidation. Before Daniela came, he hadn't minded Brent's constant filming. Now it seemed unbearably invasive. He didn't want the camera on his face while he made cow eyes at his ex-wife; he knew his longing was transparent.

After they reached the tower, Brent set up his tripod in a calm, leisurely fashion. To Sean, he seemed more like a casual observer than a director. The footage he collected was rarely prompted, and he asked few questions.

He just sort of waited for stuff to happen.

Most members of the media were impatient types, always rushing, so Sean appreciated Brent's relaxed style. Shark research was all about waiting.

Sean continued to do a slow sweep of the waters surrounding the island. He'd divided the seascape into sections, checking them off one by one. Perfect Wave, West Side, Skull Rock, North Tip. There was a flock of cormorants in the air near the bird blind, not an uncommon sight. Maybe they had their eye on a sick pup.

Often, scavengers were the first indication of a shark attack. If they'd been flying over the surface of the water, wings flapping frantically, he'd have looked closer. A lazy circle over land didn't garner a second glance.

When he was finished, he dropped his binoculars.

Jason stood next to Sean, situating himself in the frame of the shot. "Brent said he'd do shark watch again this afternoon."

Sean muttered his thanks. Offering to take Dani on a tour had been a mistake, but he couldn't change his mind now.

"Anything you want us to talk about?" Jason asked.

Brent shrugged. "Waves. Sharks. Whatever."

Jason put his hand on Sean's shoulder, nodding in the direction of the Perfect Wave. She was in fine form this morning. "Eight-to-ten, you think?"

"At least," Sean said, smiling.

"You ever paddled out in double overheads?"

"All the time."

"Maverick's?"

Sean laughed off the question, shaking his head in regret. He'd surfed some big waves before, but Maverick's was huge. The infamous spot in Northern California was for daredevils only. "Have you?"

"Just once. I got grinded."

"Lucky you didn't die."

"Yeah. But I love being able to say I tried it."

No one had ever tried the Perfect Wave, and Sean knew how much Jason wanted to. His own mouth watered for a taste of it. When he was near the ocean, he liked to surf every day. Going for weeks without his favorite sport was difficult, but he'd become accustomed to denying himself pleasure.

He was an expert in abstinence.

Talking about the Perfect Wave had become a morning ritual for them. Maybe it was pointless and immature, like bragging about women.

"What would you take out there?" Jason asked.

"Today? A short, for sure."

"Yeah. Me too."

"There's a shortboard in the supply closet," Brent commented.

Surfboards were very useful in shark research, so they always had a few on hand. Because of the time they spent in the water, surfers were the most likely victims of shark attacks. Sean had experimented with several different shapes, sizes and colors, trying to discover if the sharks had a preference. As far as he could tell, they'd bite anything. Many of the boards had chunks missing, but some were intact.

The shortboard Brent mentioned was a recent donation, and it promised a nice ride. Both Jason and Sean had both already expressed an interest in testing it.

Jason gave the Wave a hungry look, moistening his lips. He was young and bold, with a lust for life and an appetite for glory. Sean knew that having Brent film the feat, and include it in his documentary, made the idea even more tempting.

"The Foundation would never let you come back," Sean pointed out. Farallon Island was a federal preserve. As government employees, they were expected to follow safety procedures and adhere to strict standards.

He didn't bother to mention the obvious, that Jason could get *eaten by a shark*.

"I have a hoodie wetsuit," he mused, glancing at Brent. "You'd have to shoot wide, and promise not to tell anyone it was me."

"Done," Brent said.

"You're out of your mind," Sean said.

"Would you tell?"

"No, but that doesn't mean you should do it!"

His eyes darkened. "Maybe you want to get the jump on me. Is that it?"

"No, you idiot. I don't want to explain to your parents that you got killed out there, showing off on a stupid dare."

Brent raised his hands, claiming innocence. "I didn't dare anyone to do anything."

"You made the suggestion," Sean said. "Footage like that would be a great addition to your documentary, and you know it."

"Let's just drop it," Brent said. "I didn't mean to cause trouble, and I don't condone reckless behavior. You two have talked about riding that wave before. I thought you were serious. My mistake."

Your mistake, my ass, Sean thought.

Jason fell silent, not bothering to draw out the argument. Sean had the sinking feeling that Brent and Jason would continue this discussion later, without him. Jason was a hardcore surfer and a damned fool. If he had his heart set on conquering the Perfect Wave, there wasn't much Sean could do to stop him.

In the meantime, Brent was determined to get something besides boasting on film. "There's another topic I'd like to address."

Jason's brows rose. "What?"

"I have this theory that life-defining moments inform our career choices. I remember the first time I held a video camera, for example. And, the other day, Sean mentioned an incident when he was young, surfing with his father."

Sean scowled, irritated with Brent for weaseling that story out of him.

"Do you have a memorable experience, related to sharks or water?" he asked Jason.

Jason rubbed a hand over his eyes. "Yeah."

"Great," Brent said, making a few adjustments to the camera. "If you can share it, that would be cool."

"My best friend drowned," Jason said slowly. "Right after high school graduation."

Sean was surprised by the admission. Jason was talkative, but not particularly open with personal details. He was a typical guy in that sense.

"We were eighteen, drunk as hell, surfing at night. I came in. He never did."

Jason glanced at him sideways, and Sean wasn't sure what to say. In his experience, nothing helped, so he kept his mouth shut.

"I was so wasted I didn't realize what happened at first. Some of the other guys we were partying with asked where he went. Then his board washed up without him."

"Do you think it was your fault?" Brent asked.

Jason made a harsh sound. "His mom sure did. His body was found on a jetty several days later. At the funeral, she wouldn't even look at me."

Sean couldn't help but think about Natalie's funeral. When they buried his daughter, he'd had trouble meeting everyone's eyes. He couldn't bear their sadness, when he could hardly stand under the weight of his own.

"I know she thought it should have been me. He was the good kid, and I was the screwup. It *was* my fault. I pressured him into partying. It was my stupid idea to go surfing. And then I came in without him, oblivious to the fact that he'd drowned."

To his credit, Brent didn't ask any more questions. He just waited.

"I almost quit surfing after that. But every time I went out, I felt better. The ocean is very important in Filipino culture. I guess I thought that if I studied it enough, I could understand it. Control it."

Brent nodded. "Being behind the camera is also about taking control, to some extent. Do you feel the same way about your work, Sean?"

Sean frowned, considering his response. There were many times in his life he'd felt powerless, and he didn't care for it. Out on the ocean, he was in his element. But was he in control? "I know we're making a difference. Learning about sharks, and why they strike, can only help to prevent future attacks. I guess you could say it's about taking control. Predicting the unpredictable. Beating the odds."

Brent must have been satisfied with his answer, because he didn't ask him to elaborate. Instead, he did a slow pan of their surroundings. Three hundred and sixty degrees of dark blue ocean and prehistoric predators lurking in the depths.

Daniela wanted to see what lay dead or dying near the shore, but the scientists only had access to certain parts of the island. Southeast Farallon was a nature preserve, and tromping all over protected land wasn't encouraged. In some circumstances, protocol allowed them to step in and care for sick animals. Most of the time, they took a hands-off approach, favoring natural selection over human interference.

Survival of the fittest wasn't for the faint of heart.

It was probably best that she didn't see any undue suffering. Witnessing a shark attack had been gruesome, but the animal had felt little or no pain. A slow, agonizing death would have been much more difficult to watch. She hoped it wasn't another skinned pup.

Daniela and Taryn continued on to the sea lion blind without Elizabeth. Once there, she forgot about the scavenging birds, and even Taryn's strained company seemed unimportant. The slotted peepholes offered a close-up view of several full-grown Stellers. Daniela loved seals and sea lions of all kinds, and she could have happily watched them bark and belch and waddle around all day.

Before she knew it, it was time to return to the house for lunch.

She felt a twinge of excitement, along with a flurry of unease, in her belly. Touring the island by boat promised to be a unique experience. Doing it with Sean, who symbolized her deepest heartache and greatest failure, would take the edge off her enjoyment.

At the end of the path, Taryn paused, looking at Daniela over her shoulder. Her pretty face was tense. She capped a hand over her forehead, using it like a shield. "I don't like seeing Sean unhappy."

Daniela felt her mouth drop open. She closed it quickly, saying nothing.

"I mean, you obviously have issues, and that's unfortunate, but—"

"You don't know anything about me," Daniela interrupted.

"I know why you came here. And I'm not fooled by your damsel in distress act."

Her stomach tightened, as if she'd been punched. "What are you talking about?"

"You want to get back with Sean."

Daniela let out a harsh laugh, brushing by her. "You couldn't be more wrong. I had no idea he was even here."

Taryn dogged her heels. "It's clear to me that he's uncomfortable around you. Your presence is creating unnecessary tension, and we don't need the drama. Why don't you reschedule your visit for another time?"

"Why don't you? If you don't like the dynamic, leave."

She gritted her teeth. "I'm not the one screwing it up."

"You're not the one in charge, either. If Jason wants to rearrange the schedule, he will. Until then, I suggest that you mind your own business." Finished with the conversation, she turned her back on Taryn and entered the house.

Sean and Jason were standing by the cabinets in the living room. They both looked over at the same time. Sean's eyes moved from Taryn's face to Daniela's. When he lingered there, Taryn let out a frustrated breath.

"Is anyone hungry?" she asked. "I was going to make sandwiches."

Jason waved Taryn off, leaning one elbow on the countertop. "We already ate. You girls go ahead."

Taryn walked into the kitchen, her spine stiff. Obviously, the sandwich offer didn't include Daniela. Although she wasn't very hungry after the unpleasant confrontation, she grabbed a snack from the pantry and sat down at the table.

"Where's Elizabeth?" Jason asked.

"She stayed at the bird blind."

He took the chair across from her, arching a brow at her cheese and fruit. "Is that all you're going to eat?"

"I had a big breakfast," she fibbed.

"Hmm."

Last night, over tea, he'd insisted she partake in a few

cookies. "If I didn't know better, I'd think you were trying to fatten me up."

His eyes roved over her appreciatively. "Why would I do that? You're perfect the way you are."

She gave him a quelling look, but it felt good to be admired.

Sean slammed the cabinet door shut, using a little more force than was necessary. Behind his back, Jason winked at her, sharing the inside joke. Daniela almost choked on the sip of water she'd just taken.

Not only was Jason making her feel welcome, he was rubbing Sean the wrong way. Perhaps it was petty to find that amusing, but she did.

When Daniela was finished with her light lunch, they left for the afternoon tour. Taryn accompanied them to the landing to operate the crane. In the past hour, the wind had picked up. It tugged at her hair as they neared the cliffs.

Sean helped Daniela climb aboard the whaler, his large hand engulfing hers. Even through her gloves, she could feel the warmth of his touch.

A few moments later, they were out on the water. Cold air whipped at her heated cheeks, enlivening her senses, and she put aside her troubles in favor of soaking up the scenery. Barren land at summer's end wasn't much to look at, but the deep blue sea on a sunny day was a beautiful sight to behold. Yesterday, overcast conditions and afternoon fog had cast a murky spell, draining the ocean of color. Today the sky was vivid and clear, stripped clean of all but the whitest, puffiest clouds.

The Pacific was in fine form as well. Waves crashed against the rocks at the shoreline, sending up an impressive spray. Farther out, away from the island, the sea was calm.

They spotted a number of California sea lions, a small

group of Northern seals and an adorable pair of frolicking sea otters, swimming right next to the boat. If she hadn't seen one with her own eyes less than twenty-four hours ago, she wouldn't have believed great white sharks lurked under this same surface.

Of course, they rarely hunted so close to the shore.

Sean stayed quiet, sharing her enjoyment in this relaxed ambience. They'd always worked well together, communicating without saying a word.

But it was easy to get along in fair weather, wasn't it? Before the accident, their marriage had been smooth sailing, with only minor ripples. Perhaps that was why they'd been so unprepared when the going got rough.

Passing the bird-watching blind on the west side, they came upon the lazy circle of cormorants, gliding through the air. Waiting. Watching.

"Can we get closer?" Daniela asked, tentative.

Jason eyed the telltale formation. "It isn't dead yet, Daniela."

"I know. And I doubt we can help. I just want to see."

He glanced at Sean, who shrugged and looked away. They both thought she was a glutton for punishment, and maybe they were right. But she knew it was important for her to acknowledge these signs of death and to face them.

Jason maneuvered the whaler into a better viewing position. Between two peaks, on a flat stretch of ground a few feet from the water's edge, there was a harbor seal cub, freckled with the signature white spots that were unique to the breed. Obviously just-weaned, he was plump from a diet of nutrient-rich milk, his speckled brown coat shiny with health.

And around his neck, the cause of his distress, was a plastic ring.

It wasn't an unusual sight. Many animals died this way every year. This kind of trash found its way into the ocean, didn't break down once it got there, and remained strong enough to suffocate and kill.

Ironically, water bottles of all sizes were the most egregious offenders.

This once-playful pup had probably stuck his head into a piece of plastic out of curiosity, and as he'd grown, the noose had tightened. Now, he was lying on his side, motionless, having outgrown the collar so quickly he could scarcely breathe.

"Do you have a knife?" she asked, measuring the distance from the boat to the crashing surf at the shore.

"We can't reach him from here," Sean said.

"He's so close! I could—"

"What?" he interrupted. "Swim to him? If you didn't get your head smashed against the rocks by waves, you still couldn't haul yourself out of the water at this location. It's too slippery, too steep and way too dangerous."

Knowing he was right, she frowned at the dying cub. Reaching him by land would take time, and some careful climbing, but it was doable. Once she got to him, it would be a simple matter of cutting away the debris.

This kind of intervention made her job intensely rewarding, and she was eager to assist the helpless pup.

"Take me back to the landing," she said, eying the crowded sky with trepidation. The flock of scavengers had grown restless, and they didn't want to wait to begin their feast. Cormorants were called the vultures of the sea for good reason.

"He's not going anywhere—"

As soon as the words were out of his mouth, a greedy bird came diving down, plucking at the animal's exposed side. He bleated weakly, unable to protect himself from their vicious onslaught. One after another, the winged predators attacked the pup, growing bolder, drawing blood.

"Damned shags," Jason muttered. "I wish I had some rocks to throw."

The young seal let out a loud bellow, whipping his head around. With a valiant effort, he heaved his body across the few feet of rock and slid off the edge, disappearing into the relative safety of the water.

Heart sinking, Daniela examined every inch of the surface, but the pup was gone.

"He'll turn back up," Jason said, making a stab at optimism. One glance at Sean told a truer tale. The only place this pup was going was a shark's belly.

She sat down on the bench and hugged her arms around herself, feeling hollow. When the seal didn't resurface, they continued on the tour, leaving the somber scene behind them.

But Daniela didn't have time to let depression set in. A moment later, the engine made a strange hissing sound. It choked, sputtered a few times and then stalled completely.

Chapter 7

Thick black smoke plumed up from the engine, and the smell of burning plastic filled Daniela's nostrils.

Sean leaped to his feet, striding to the back of the boat to inspect the damage.

"What the hell," Jason muttered, hitting some switches on the dash before he joined Sean at the stern. There must have been a manual override, because he tried to restart the engine by hand. He yanked the cord, but it didn't turn over.

Daniela's stomach dropped. "What's wrong?"

Jason tried again and again. Nothing happened. "It's dead."

"Oars," Sean said, scrambling to open a storage compartment in the floor. He threw out a couple of orange life vests and a length of yellow rope, his hands searching. The notches that normally housed the oars were empty. "Did you take them out?"

Jason paled. "No."

Sean thrust a hand through his hair, cursing fluently. They were only a hundred feet from shore, at the most. And it may as well have been a hundred miles. "This is unbelievable! Who would remove the oars?"

Jason picked up his radio, calling Brent at the tower. "We have a problem."

Brent responded immediately. "What's up?"

"No engine, no oars."

"Copy that," he said. "Should I call in an SOS? Surely there's a boat nearby."

Jason deliberated for a moment, exchanging a dark glance with Sean. Commercial ships and private vessels cruised in and out of the bay at all hours, but once the whaler drifted away from the island, she would be hard to spot.

Without GPS, even the Coast Guard would have trouble finding them. They could be stranded indefinitely.

"Screw this," Sean said, yanking his sweater over his head. His T-shirt came with it. Bare-chested, he sat down to take off his boots.

Daniela felt the air rush out of her lungs. "What are you doing?"

He ignored her. "How much rope do we have?"

"Two fifties," Jason answered.

"Tie them together."

Jason secured the two fifty-foot ropes together in a fisherman's knot while Sean made a loop at one end.

"No," Daniela breathed, measuring the distance to the shore. "You'll never make it."

"She's right," Jason said. "I should go."

Sean brought the loop over his head and arm, sling-style, so that it lay diagonally across his chest. "Why?"

He gestured at Daniela. "I don't have a—"

Sean's eyes locked on hers. "Neither do I."

Every moment, they were drifting farther out. By the time he reached shore, there was no telling how far out the boat would be.

"Don't do this," she pleaded.

Sean jerked his chin toward the open sea. "Do you want to take our chances out there? At night?"

"Oh God," she moaned, unable to fathom that fate.

"Go," Jason said, making the choice for them. "Or I will."

Sean didn't have to be told twice. He dove off the end of the boat, cutting into the ocean like a knife. As soon as he surfaced, he began swimming toward the shore, his movements strong and sure. The water temperature must have been bitterly cold, because she could see the steam rising from his body. His shoulder muscles rippled in the afternoon light, shining wet and sharply defined.

Jason tied off the other end of the rope, giving as much slack as he could spare. He stayed in radio communication with Brent, but Daniela wasn't aware of the actual words spoken. Her entire focus was on Sean.

He sliced through the water in powerful strokes, eating up the distance to the shore. Despite the chilly temperature, which robbed the body of energy and turned muscles into sludge, his crawl was well-executed and his pace steady.

Even so, she was frozen with fear for him.

From her research, Daniela knew there was an invisible ring around the island that the scientists called the Red Circle. It denoted a specific depth and distance from shore in which the incidence of shark attack was much higher. This area often corresponded with a steep drop-off or other underwater features sharks used for cover.

Seals and sea lions crossing this space exercised extreme caution, rarely swimming on the surface of the water.

And Sean was passing right through it.

Yesterday, they'd watched a shark devour a 500-pound sea lion less than a mile from this very spot.

She almost couldn't bear to watch.

"He'll make it," Jason said.

Daniela's heart was pounding against her chest, her pulse thundering in her ears. No sharks, her mind screamed. Please, God, no sharks.

"He's going to make it," Jason repeated, sounding more certain. "He's almost there."

The last few feet took the most effort. Sean's rope stretched across the distance, taking up the slack. When he reached a rocky area near the bird blind, he struggled to haul himself out of the water, but the rope over his shoulder stayed taut.

The current was pulling him backward.

"Come on," Jason urged.

Finally, Sean dragged himself out of the water, his muscles straining for every inch. He lay on the rocky shore for a moment, catching his breath. The rope tugged at him, threatening to yank him back into the water.

"He can't bring us in," Daniela said.

"No," Jason agreed. "He's going to anchor us. We'll pull ourselves in."

Easier said than done. There was a jagged rock near Sean, pointing up toward the sky. He slipped the rope off his shoulder and widened the loop, trying to make it fit over the rock. This took several tries, and extreme care, as the rope had a lot of tension.

If it slipped from his hands, all would be lost.

On the last try, he managed to slide the loop down over the jagged rock. It held tight, anchoring them to shore.

Jason gave a celebratory shout, pumping his fist in the air. "Yes!"

Daniela was right there with him, hugging his side and laughing, tears of relief streaming down her face.

At the shore, Sean lay flat on his back, panting.

"I'm going to need your help," Jason warned, testing the rope.

Daniela wasn't a physics master, but she understood that they had to use leverage to bring themselves in. When Jason started pulling, leaning back with his body weight, she wrapped her arms around his taut waist and heaved, adding her weight to his.

Jason wasn't as big as Sean, and Daniela was small, even for a woman, but they both gave it their all. It took every ounce of their combined strength to get started. After a grueling initial effort, they made forward progress. The boat crept toward the shore, little by little. Jason's hands moved across the rope, end over end.

Daniela was able to release his waist and grab the rope, helping Jason pull them in. Her arms shook from exertion, and sweat broke out on her forehead as they gained momentum. Together, they made it to shore.

The next few minutes took on a surreal, dreamlike quality. Sean tied off the whaler and Jason helped her ashore. They waded through waist-high water and scrambled onto slippery rock. She'd never felt happier to be on land. Breathing hard and soaking wet, she lay back and stared up at the cold blue sky, giddy from relief and exhaustion.

When he'd recovered well enough to talk, Jason gave Sean a surfer handshake. "That was awesome, dude. You're my hero."

Sean laughed, shielding his eyes from the sun with his forearm.

Daniela knew both men were riding high on adrenaline,

and so was she, but she didn't find anything humorous about the situation. Sean could have been killed. A moment ago, she'd been paralyzed with fear, crying her eyes out.

And they thought it was funny?

Sean caught a glimpse of her face and sobered. "Are you okay?"

"I'm fine." Despite her feelings of hurt and confusion, her heart filled with another, more tender emotion. She wanted to wrap her arms around his neck and press her lips to his throat. She wanted to hold on tight and never let him go.

Instead, she sat up, drawing her knees to her chest. She realized that he'd risked his life because of her. He knew she couldn't handle drifting out to sea. She'd have gone mad, stuck in a tiny boat, surrounded by a vast ocean.

Maybe Taryn was right. Her presence here created drama, conflict—even danger.

"What do you think happened to the engine?" Sean asked.

Jason shrugged. "I don't know. It looks pretty thrashed."

"Do you have an extra?"

"Yeah. In the utility shed."

Elizabeth and Taryn came scrambling over the rocks, their voices carrying on the wind. Brent followed close behind, a set of oars resting on one broad shoulder.

Their appearance felt like an interruption. Daniela needed some time with Jason and Sean, to process what happened. Over the course of the afternoon, and the past few harrowing moments, the three of them had bonded. Jason had become her friend.

And Sean would always be…something more.

As if in direct opposition to her thoughts, he rose to his

feet, eager to greet the others. And Taryn rushed forward, launching herself into Sean's arms.

Their embrace didn't look platonic. She splayed her hands across his bare shoulders, plastering her slender body full-length against his. They fit together perfectly, a golden couple in the afternoon sun.

"That was amazing," Brent said, his eyes bright with excitement. "I think I got it all on film, too. I left the camera at the tower rolling."

Daniela pictured this scene in his documentary, fading to black after a romantic, aesthetically pleasing last frame, and she felt sharp pain in the center of her chest. She turned her face toward the horizon, telling herself it was only anxiety.

Sean didn't know what the hell Daniela wanted.

One moment, she seemed relieved he'd made it out of the water alive. The next, she was looking at him like she wished he'd died.

It wasn't as if he expected her to be overwhelmed with joy and throw herself at his feet, confessing that she still cared. But they'd been married, and he would always love her, so the evidence of her apathy didn't just crush his ego.

It hurt, all the way down to his soul.

Maybe she thought he should have let Jason go instead of him. Although they were equally good swimmers, Sean was taller and more muscular. He'd been able to bring the rope to shore, so there was no reason for Jason to risk his life.

He understood that Daniela was sensitive to high-pressure situations, and he hadn't meant to distress her, but he couldn't let the whaler drift out to sea. The idea of her being stranded all night, struggling not to panic, had been unbearable.

He would protect her from that kind of trauma at any cost.

Besides that, it felt good to save the day. Damned good. He'd do it again in a heartbeat. He'd do it a thousand times over. He only wished he'd been able to come to Dani's rescue two years ago, when she'd really needed him.

He'd never forgive himself for letting her down. Playing the hero this time didn't erase his guilt, or make him forget about all the mistakes he'd made in the past, but it helped to soothe a raw place inside of him.

Taryn's embrace soothed him further.

She wasn't the one he wanted to hold the most, but he enjoyed having a woman in his arms and his feet on the ground.

"I thought you were going to get killed," Taryn said, her hands on his face. "I thought a shark would eat you."

"I'd be a poor meal for a white, after a diet of fat sea lions."

"True," she said with a teary smile, smoothing her palms over his shoulders. "You're all muscle and bone."

He didn't want to give Taryn the wrong impression, so he let her go. He'd held her a little too close, for a little too long. Sharing an innocent hug with her was no big deal, and Taryn didn't mean anything by it, but maybe *his* motives were suspect.

Using her to make Daniela jealous was pathetic. Not to mention futile.

"They probably wouldn't come back for more than one bite," Jason agreed. "But you'd still bleed to death."

It was a common misconception that white sharks were indiscriminate diners. Although they would investigate almost anything, and rip it to shreds in the process, they usually wouldn't continue to feed on lean meat. It was unknown whether attacks on humans were the result of mistaken identity or idle curiosity, but man was not part of their preferred diet.

Unfortunately, an exploratory bite from a great white was often fatal.

One glance at Daniela revealed her concern. Her face was pinched and pale, her eyes dark with emotion.

She *had* been worried about him. And he'd comforted Taryn instead of her. Feeling like an insensitive bastard, he faltered, fumbling for the right words to make it better. As was all too common in his experience, they wouldn't come.

So he scowled at Jason. "Was that observation really necessary?"

Jason shrugged, taking the oars from Brent. "Let's get back to the landing so I can take a look at the engine."

Jason was angry with him now, too, which figured. He'd wanted the starring role in Brent's documentary—a part Sean had just stolen from him, unwittingly. And, perhaps because his attraction to Elizabeth wasn't going anywhere, Jason also seemed interested in trying out for Daniela's leading man.

This level of competition could generate some real hard feelings between them.

While the others walked back to the house, Sean and Jason stayed behind to take care of the whaler. It couldn't be left at this location without sustaining serious damage to the hull. Sean untied the ropes and they waded through the water, climbing aboard once again.

Rowing the boat back to the landing wasn't easy. In wet clothes, they were cold and uncomfortable. After pulling the whaler in, Jason's arms must have been burning from exertion, and Sean was tired after a hard swim, but neither of them complained.

"These oars are from the supply shed," Sean commented.

"Yep."

"Any idea where the original ones went?"

"Nope."

"When did you check them last?"

"I counted the life jackets last week, but I don't remember noticing the oars. There's no reason to remove them."

"Maybe one got broken, and someone meant to replace the set, but forgot."

Jason grunted a noncommittal response, rowing harder over the last stretch. Sean shut up and followed suit. The feat should have boosted his spirits, but it hadn't. Knowing the toll his actions had taken on Daniela, he only felt... numb.

The instant they returned to the house, he went upstairs and changed into dry clothes. As he headed back down the hall, he noticed that the door to Daniela and Taryn's room was slightly ajar.

He paused, rapping his knuckles against it. "Dani?"

"I'm on my way out," she said, her voice husky.

He ducked his head in. "Can I talk to you?"

"Of course." Her eyes were dark and luminous, her hair wind-tossed and her cheeks flushed from the time spent outdoors. She sat down at the desk with her hands in her lap, waiting for him to speak.

There were no other chairs, so he took a seat on the lower bunk, hunching his back to keep from hitting his head against the upper frame. It was awkward, but it wasn't as bad as towering over her.

The situation reminded him of their counseling sessions.

For six months after the accident, they'd gone to a grief specialist. At the end of each session, the therapist had asked him to turn toward Dani for "sharing time." Sean had always made eye contact and listened carefully, but he'd never known what to say.

"I'm sorry," he said, moving his gaze from her clasped hands to her beautiful face.

She moistened her lips. "For what?"

In the past, his answer might have been, "For whatever I did wrong," or, even better, "For upsetting you." While perfectly acceptable, in his mind, those responses hadn't gone over well with her. This time, he dug a little deeper and told her what he was really sorry about. "For not being there for you," he said, meeting her eyes.

She didn't have to ask what he meant. Tilting her head to one side, she asked, "What do you think you could have done?"

"Taken your place," he said immediately. "You shouldn't have been driving."

Her brows drew together. "I suppose you think you could have avoided the SUV spinning out of control across the freeway."

"No. I meant I wish it had been me. I wish I'd been hurt, instead of you. I'd have done anything to take your pain."

"Sean—" She broke off, squeezing her eyes shut. The tears spilled out anyway, wetting her thick lashes.

He knew he was screwing this up, the same way he had everything else. His own throat tightened, because the last thing he wanted to do was hurt her again. But he continued, needing to have his say. "I'm also sorry if you were scared while I was out in the water. I know what it's like to go crazy with worry. When you were in the hospital, I went through hell."

"Yes," she murmured, drying her wet cheek with one shirtsleeve. "Taryn told me how distraught you were. Did you cry on her shoulder?"

Actually, he'd cried in her lap, but he didn't want Daniela to know that. He was ashamed of his helplessness, his loss of control and lack of strength. God, he'd been a wreck after the accident. He was glad she hadn't seen him like that.

"There's nothing between Taryn and me," he said, feeling heat creep up his neck.

She stared at him, probably wondering why he would say that. He didn't know himself. Letting her believe he was involved with Taryn had been a defense mechanism, an attempt to hide the truth from her.

He would always feel vulnerable around Daniela.

The day she'd signed the divorce papers had been the second worst of his life. Even now, a year later, his gut clenched at the memory. The torn-up pieces of his heart had just begun to knit together, and every moment he spent with her tested the seams.

She moistened her lips, looking up at him with big brown eyes.

Sean pulled his gaze away, his chest tight with longing. He still wanted her, but he wouldn't act on it. If he did, she would withdraw from him. Turn to the side, twist out of his arms, avoid his touch.

He had to stop fantasizing about getting back together with her, and torturing himself by imagining passionate make-up scenarios. It was time to face the facts. She wasn't going to melt in his arms, sobbing that she couldn't live without him.

She would never arch her luscious body against his, rake her nails down his back or pant softly into his ear.

If he reached for her, she would only pull away again.

Chapter 8

They didn't watch the footage until after dinner.

Jason and Sean spent several hours switching out the engines. Brent used the time to do some rough editing, Elizabeth transferred her handwritten research notes to her laptop and Taryn made a couple of pizzas.

Still reeling from the boat accident, and her subsequent conversation with Sean, Daniela immersed herself in work, writing a detailed log of the Steller sea lions she'd observed that day. From what she'd seen, the population was thriving. Tomorrow, she would do a comprehensive head count, and take blood samples to send to the lab.

At the end of the evening, they gathered around the television to watch Brent's "home movie." Daniela wasn't looking forward to reliving the incident, or seeing herself on film, but it would be cowardly to decline.

She'd come here to face her fears, not run from them.

She took a seat next to Elizabeth, who also seemed

reluctant to watch. Her posture was stiff and her lips were pursed with displeasure. Taryn, on the other hand, was totally relaxed, curled up on the other side of the couch. Sean lounged on the floor nearby, his forearm propped up on one bent knee, his back resting against the cushioned frame.

Ready to see some action, Jason had sprawled out in the middle of the floor, his hands braced behind his head.

Brent knelt next to the TV, cueing up the clip. "This is a very rough cut," he warned. "Like watching dailies."

"Just play it," Jason said. "We don't even know what dailies are."

Brent seemed excited about sharing his vision with them. His boyish enthusiasm made Daniela smile.

He pressed play, and the footage started in an unexpected place, with a conversation between Jason and Sean. Daniela had to admit, Brent knew what he was doing. The natural lighting was superb, his subjects were handsome and the backdrop was spectacular.

In one frame, he'd captured the harsh beauty of the island and the rugged appeal of two of its very charismatic inhabitants.

This was no ordinary documentary.

Jason had his hand on Sean's shoulder, and they were admiring something in the distance. Their body language suggested they were discussing a beautiful woman, and she felt a pang of longing, wanting to *be* that woman.

A few seconds later, she realized they were talking about the Perfect Wave. Sean wasn't discouraging Jason from riding it, either. On the contrary, he seemed intent on tasting a slice of that pie himself.

Beside her, Elizabeth clenched her hands into fists.

Daniela waited for Sean and Jason to say they were only joking, but that didn't happen. Jason shared a serious story about a friend who'd drowned, and the scene ended with a wide shot of the breaking wave.

Elizabeth rose to her feet. "I can't believe you! Your best friend dies, so you want to follow him? And you—" She pointed a finger at Sean, narrowing her eyes. "You promised you wouldn't encourage him."

Sean straightened to defend himself. "I promised I wouldn't *help* him. There's a difference."

She threw her hands in the air.

"Sean did try to talk me out of it," Jason explained, "and this tricky bastard cut that part out of the footage."

Brent smiled wryly, guilty as charged.

She crossed her arms over her chest. "Did he cut the part where you said you weren't going to do it, too?"

"Not exactly," he said, rubbing a hand over his jaw.

Elizabeth had heard enough. She grabbed her knapsack off the table and started toward the staircase.

"Keep this up, and I'll be fooled into thinking you care," Jason murmured.

Without so much as a backward glance, she went upstairs.

"Maybe I shouldn't play the rest," Brent said.

Taryn waved a dismissive hand in the air. "Don't worry about her. I can't wait to see it. Some of us *like* a little excitement." With a pointed glance at Daniela, she smoothed her palm over Sean's shoulder, giving him a comforting squeeze.

Brent looked from Sean to Taryn to Daniela, catching every nuance. The situation was so awkward it was painful. *Just show the damned clip,* she urged Brent silently. As soon as it was over, she could leave.

The next scene began with Jason's emergency call. After responding on his radio, Brent zoomed in, getting a tight shot of the three of them inside the boat. There was a moment of chaos, reflected in the choppy images and lack of focus.

A sudden close-up revealed Daniela's face in exquisite detail. Her expression betrayed a wealth of fear and anguish.

Sean sucked in a sharp breath, and Taryn's hand fell away from his shoulder.

It was difficult for Daniela to look at herself on the screen. She saw eyes that were too big, too dark, too expressive.

Her terror was so magnified, it was almost grotesque.

Thankfully, the shot widened, and Sean took his shirt off, stealing the scene. His skin was darkly tanned, his stomach corrugated with muscle. There was no denying that he looked fantastic. Like her frightened face, this image was powerful and provocative. Together, they made an odd juxtaposition—his raw sexuality, and her unadulterated fear.

As he began to swim, the shot cut from Sean to the boat and back again, catching her distress and Jason's support, creating the same tension she'd felt during the initial experience. Finally, Sean climbed out of the water, his chest heaving. His wet jeans clung to his thighs, riding so low on his abdomen that an inch of his pubic hair was exposed.

"Wow," Taryn said, enjoying the view.

Daniela had to admit, she was just as riveted. Sean's biceps flexed as he strained forward with the rope, his teeth clenched from exertion. Only Jason seemed unfazed by the display of skin and strength.

Sean arched a brow at Brent. "It didn't occur to you to put down the camera and come help us?"

"I never would have got there in time. So I waited to see if you made it."

"Convenient," Sean muttered, turning his attention back to the footage.

Once the boat was anchored, Brent left the tower. After that, the shot stayed wide and didn't change. She and Jason pulled in the whaler, foot by foot. It was an exciting sequence. At the end, the three of them lay together on the wet rocks, exhausted.

Daniela almost couldn't bear to watch Taryn and Sean's embrace, which appeared even more romantic from a distance.

She expected heartache, not surprise. She got both. Before the gorgeous couple broke apart, a flash of movement caught her eye. There was a dark shape in the water, about a hundred feet from shore.

A fin.

"Oh my God," she gasped, clapping a hand over her mouth. None of them had noticed the shark at the time.

Its presence elevated an already compelling scene to cinematic gold.

"Did you splice that in?" Sean asked.

Brent smiled. "I'm good, but I'm not that good."

Taryn was also disturbed by the footage. Shuddering, she slipped her arms around Sean's neck and dropped a kiss on the top of his head.

It was a telling gesture, like the belly-to-belly embrace they'd shared earlier, and Daniela had seen enough. Sean claimed he wasn't involved in a relationship with Taryn, but they didn't act like "just friends."

She rose from the couch, hoping for steady legs. "I'm off to bed."

Brent appeared hurt by her abrupt departure. Perhaps he'd expected his footage to inspire joy and wonderment, rather than shock and awe. "Can we do a short interview? I meant to catch you last night, and didn't get a chance."

"Sure," she said, her shoulders sagging. "Where?"

"In my room. It will only take a minute."

Jason got up to say good night to her, but he seemed distracted. He hadn't spoken since Elizabeth left the room.

Sean's gaze met hers, his expression inscrutable. "Good night," he said gruffly.

"Sweet dreams," Taryn murmured, her arms still twined around his neck.

Brent's room was tiny.

It boasted a single bed that couldn't have been long enough for his six-foot-plus frame, and a small armchair. Behind the chair, there was a blank screen; in front of it, a high-watt lamp. His camera stand was already set up near the bed.

"Have a seat," he said.

She did, twisting her hands in her lap.

"I need to close the door."

"Go ahead," she said, smiling at his politeness.

The room was so cramped he couldn't even sit down on the edge of the bed to turn on his camera until he'd shut the door. She fidgeted with her hair while he played with the settings, wishing she'd thought to put on a little makeup.

"Are you camera-shy?"

"No," she said quickly. "No, I—" She caught the look on his face and gave up. "Yes. Yes, of course I am. I suppose it's obvious."

It was his turn to smile. "Not really."

"You're a terrible liar."

He laughed, glancing through the viewfinder and making one last adjustment. "There's no reason to be nervous. The camera loves you."

She shrugged off the compliment. "I bet you say that to all the girls."

"No. Taryn photographs well, but she doesn't have your eyes. You remind me of a silent film star. Very expressive."

Heat rose to her cheeks. She felt tired and worn-down, rather than pretty.

"Tell me about yourself. What draws you to this line of work? Why seals?"

Daniela took a deep breath. "I was born in Sinaloa, Mexico. It's on the Pacific Coast, south of Baja. My father was a fisherman, and he took me to work with him fairly often. I loved to swim. He called me *foquita*. Little seal."

He waited for her to continue.

"There aren't many seals that far south, but we kept an eye out for them. He told me about the *foca del caribe*. Caribbean monk seal. They've been extinct since the 1950s."

"And that left an impression on you?"

"Oh, yes. I didn't believe him at first. I couldn't imagine how an entire species could be wiped out. From then on, I wanted to learn more about endangered animals. Conservation biology seemed like a perfect fit."

"Where did you go to school?"

"In San Diego. We moved there when I was ten."

"Did your father continue to fish?"

She hesitated for a moment, surprised by the question. "No, he didn't. My mother came from a wealthy, aristocratic family, and she wanted the best for us. Fishing didn't pay enough to suit her. He went to night school and got a degree in finance."

"Did that pay enough?"

Daniela shrugged. Mamá was impossible to please.

"How did the change suit him?"

"Not very well," she admitted. "He was much happier in his fishing days. It was almost as if he'd left a piece of his soul out there, on the water." She smiled sadly, remembering the last time she'd seen him.

"Foquita," he always said, wrapping his arms around her. *"No nades tan lejos."*

Don't swim so far away.

Since the accident, their relationship had been stilted. For months, she'd avoided his company, not wanting comfort from anyone. That day, he'd hugged her warily, as if he were afraid she might break.

"I'm sorry," she said, blinking back tears.

Brent turned the camera off. "Don't be. I shouldn't have kept you up this late. It's been a difficult day."

"You're very kind."

"No. Right now, I'm thinking about how beautiful you are, and how great this footage will look in my documentary."

And yet, out of respect to her, he'd stopped filming. "Thank you."

He grabbed a tissue for her, from the box on the nightstand. Daniela noticed a framed photograph resting next to it. "Is that your girlfriend?" she asked, accepting the tissue and dabbing her eyes.

"Yeah." He picked up the photograph and handed it to her.

The woman in the picture was pretty, but frail-looking. She wore a colorful scarf over her dark hair, and she was much too slender.

"She has cancer," he explained.

Daniela almost dropped the frame. "Oh, I—I'm so sorry."

"It's in remission, or I wouldn't have come. I'm hoping to film here a few weeks, and get back home to do the editing. I like to be with her as much as possible. We don't know how much time she has."

She handed him the photo, struck by the tragedy of his situation. Hearing about it put her troubles in perspective. She also couldn't help but feel guilty. She was alive, and recovering, while his girlfriend was dying.

He interrupted her thoughts. "Shall we finish this tomorrow?"

She nodded, leaving the room after saying a quiet good night. It *had* been a difficult day. Her arms ached from pulling rope and her palms burned. Feeling like a zombie, she stumbled into her room.

Taryn wasn't there.

She was probably downstairs, on the couch with Sean. Kissing his hard mouth. Touching all those lovely muscles. Sitting in his lap.

Telling herself it didn't matter, and that she didn't care, Daniela climbed into bed and turned off the lamp. The night-light in the corner flickered gaily, mocking her solitude. Because it belonged to Taryn, she wanted to smash it to bits.

Instead, she turned her face to the wall and stared, wide-eyed, into darkness.

Sean pulled Taryn's arms off his neck and rose to his feet. "We have to talk."

Her surprised expression sent up a warning flag. She hadn't been acting touchy-feely just to irritate Daniela. And what she'd been expecting from him, right now, was a lot more intimate than conversation.

He smothered a groan, calling himself ten kinds of stupid.

She got up off the couch with a small frown, grabbing her jacket and following him out the front door. There was no guaranteed privacy downstairs, and he wasn't about to take her to his room. Jason was still fooling around with the old engine in the equipment shed, so Sean walked in the other direction.

It was the same place he'd stood last night, staring out at Skull Rock.

He didn't think he'd encouraged Taryn, and damned if he knew how to discourage her. She was a fun girl, like a cute kid sister.

This was…weird.

"We're friends, right?" he said.

"Of course."

"Just friends."

Her eyes sparkled in the moonlight. "Is that what you want?"

"Yes."

Smiling a little, she stepped forward, closing the distance between them. "Are you sure?" she whispered, touching her lips to his ear.

He would have backed up, but they were at the edge of the cliffs, and there was nowhere to go but down. "I'm sure," he said, turning his head to one side.

Undeterred by his insistence, she wrapped her arms around his neck and pressed kisses along his jaw.

Although he was more annoyed than interested, he allowed her to continue. He hadn't received this kind of attention from a woman in years. Ironically, Daniela's arrival made him susceptible to Taryn's wiles. After spending most of the afternoon with his lovely ex-wife, he was very aware of his physical needs.

She slid her hand over the front of his pants, testing his resolve.

Sean knew a moment of male weakness. Taryn wasn't the one he wanted, but she was hot and willing. More than willing. Unlike Daniela, she wouldn't push him away. In fact, he was pretty certain she'd do anything he liked.

That was tempting.

"Let's go up to the tower," she said, breathless. Her tongue touched his earlobe as her fingers clenched around him.

Gritting his teeth, he removed her hand. "No."

Startled by his vehemence, she stumbled back a step, and he used that opportunity to put some space between them. He turned to face the Pacific, focusing on the crashing waves, feeling the cold wind on his face.

"Is it because she's here?"

"No," he said, and it was the truth. Daniela's presence made this scene twice as tawdry, but he wouldn't have slept with Taryn under different circumstances. Not with a committed relationship in mind, anyway. She was too young, too easy, too…uncomplicated.

They didn't have anything in common.

"Are you still in love with her?"

He sighed, shaking his head. It was more avoidance than denial.

"You're a fool," she decided, her voice gritty with emotion. "She'll only hurt you."

He glanced at her sideways, wondering if he'd underestimated her capacity for being vindictive, along with her amorous intentions. Daniela didn't need any more grief from Taryn. Tomorrow, he'd talk to Dani about leaving again.

"I can't have you making trouble for Daniela," he said. "Touching me in front of her, or acting…too familiar."

She let out a frustrated breath, visible in the night air. "It's okay for you to put your hands all over me, playing football or whatever, but I can't give you a hug?"

Sean hadn't realized that she'd misinterpreted the

physical contact. If he'd known she had a crush on him, he wouldn't have roughhoused with her. "I'm sorry if I gave you the wrong impression."

"We've had a connection from the start."

His gut clenched with apprehension. "What do you mean?"

"Even before Daniela's accident, I felt it. I know you felt it, too."

"I was *married*."

"That's why I didn't do anything about it."

"Taryn, I would never have touched you back then. The only connection we've ever had is friendship."

Her face went slack with shock. "Fine," she said, her lips trembling. "I really thought— I mean, I was sure you— never mind."

"I'm sorry," he repeated, knowing he'd hurt her. "It's not that I don't find you attractive. Obviously, I do. You're a beautiful girl, and I like you as a friend. But I wouldn't choose to take it further."

She gave him a brittle smile. "Gotcha."

He shoved his hands into his pockets, feeling like an asshole. That was what he should have said *before* she started kissing him.

"You go on ahead," she said, nodding toward the front door. "I just need a minute."

At that moment, Brent came outside to smoke. He didn't glance in their direction as he shut the door behind him. Minding his own business, he leaned against the side of the house, cupped a hand around his face to block the wind and lit up.

Sean wondered at his timing. For a guy who was supposedly here to shoot a scientific documentary, he sure had a nose for drama.

"I'll see you tomorrow," he muttered to Brent, trying

to roll the tension out of his shoulders as he walked back inside the house. Over the past few hours, he'd crushed Taryn's ego, put Dani through hell and upset Elizabeth.

Time to call it a day, before he did any more damage.

Chapter 9

Daniela stayed awake late, torturing herself with images of Sean and Taryn, writhing all over each other. She must have drifted off in the wee hours of the morning, because she didn't remember hearing the girl come in.

As Daniela opened her eyes, Taryn was sitting in the chair across from the bed, brushing her damp hair. Her eyes were puffy and her mouth drawn. The room smelled like honeysuckle.

Daniela sat up in bed, blinking groggily.

Taryn placed the brush on the surface of the desk with a quiet click. "Yesterday, when I said you should leave, I was out of line. I apologize."

"Apology accepted," she said, surprised.

"That was unprofessional, not to mention unkind. It won't happen again."

"Don't worry about it," she murmured.

With a stiff nod, Taryn rose from the chair, turning her

attention to the oval mirror on the wall behind the desk. She looked tanned and trim in low-rise jeans and a fitted sweater that left a few inches of her flat belly exposed. Frowning at her reflection, she parted her hair into two sections and began to braid it.

Taryn had the kind of figure Daniela had always envied. Long legs, slender proportions and a lithe upper body. She could probably buy any shirt off the rack and have it fit. By the looks of it, she didn't even need to wear a bra.

Daniela hadn't been able to get away with that since the sixth grade.

Annoyed by Taryn's youthful perkiness, she wrestled out of her sleeping bag. After leaving the warmth of her bed, she changed her clothes in a hurry, shivering from cold. The jeans she chose were old and comfortable, but the long-sleeved top must have shrunk in the wash, because it fit too snugly across the chest. A small row of buttons, halfway down the front, strained to hold in her assets.

Sighing, she rummaged through the rest of her clothes. Luckily, she'd brought a striped scarf. She'd be wearing her jacket all day, anyway, but the scarf would keep her modestly covered until she went outside.

As she draped the scarf around her neck, she noticed Taryn watching her out of the corner of her eye. Her expression wasn't smug and sultry, like last night. Nor did she seem satisfied about her tryst with Sean.

Instead, she appeared to be burning with resentment. Had he asked her to apologize?

Downstairs, the mood was equally forced. Taryn ignored Daniela and avoided Sean. Elizabeth was more aloof than ever. Even Jason seemed tense.

"Looks like rain," Brent commented, staring out the front window.

"We have to scrub the catchment pad today," Jason said.

He glanced around the room, as if expecting a chorus of groans. No one said a word.

Brent seemed amused by the strained atmosphere. "I'll help," he said. "Unless you want me to do shark watch."

"No. It's a labor-intensive job, and we could use the extra muscle."

"I can't promise much of that, being more brains than brawn." He cast a sideways glance at Sean and smiled.

Obviously, Sean had plenty of both.

Daniela pictured him climbing out of the surf yesterday, his chest bare and his pants wet. Although he was comfortable with his body, he'd always been dismissive—even embarrassed—about his good looks. He was probably horrified by the fact that Brent had made the footage of him look like a cologne commercial.

Clearing his throat, he left the table.

After the breakfast dishes were done, they grabbed a few buckets and some wire-bristled brushes out of the supply closet. The cement catchment pad was only a few hundred yards from the house. Apparently, gulls used it as roosting grounds during the summer. It was covered with feathers and filth.

Southeast Farallon Island was a "green" research facility, powered by solar energy, environmentally friendly and self-sufficient in many ways. Accordingly, all of the water they used for drinking and washing was collected on the catchment pad during heavy rains. The water was filtered and stored in an aboveground cistern, but it wasn't treated or purified.

Cleaning the catchment pad before the first big rain was essential.

And, judging by the sky, a serious storm was coming. Bruised clouds crept in from the Pacific, darkening the edges of the horizon.

Daniela knew that the island was infamous for extreme weather. During a really powerful storm, charter boats couldn't bring supplies in from the mainland—or take anyone back. This might be her last chance to chicken out.

"When do you think it will hit?" Brent asked Sean, looking up at the sky.

"Tonight, maybe. Sometimes they pass on by, this early in the season."

Jason was right about the catchment pad; it was a dirty job, and scrubbing the cement required a lot of upper body strength. The gunk on the surface looked nasty, smelled bad and had the consistency of dried plaster.

After less than thirty minutes, Daniela was sweating. The men had already stripped down to their T-shirts, and there was a pile of discarded jackets next to the catchment pad. Finally, she took off her jacket *and* her wool scarf, both of which kept getting in the way.

Jason and Sean worked tirelessly, covering twice as much area as the rest of them combined. The girls slowed down a bit, but they didn't complain. Although her biceps felt sore from yesterday's tug on the rope, Daniela was determined to do her part. She continued scrubbing, her eyes downcast.

An hour later, Sean broke the silence. "If you're going to point the camera down Daniela's shirt, you could at least ask her permission first."

She looked up, startled. Brent had taken a break, and turned on his ubiquitous camera.

"I was filming Taryn, not Daniela," he explained.

Taryn was on her hands and knees, with her back to the camera. Her taut backside was barely covered by her low-rise jeans, and Brent had taken advantage of that photo op.

She glanced over her shoulder, arching a brow at Sean. "I don't mind."

"Well, I do," Elizabeth said, giving him a cold stare. "Are you shooting for a wildlife documentary or a Calvin Klein ad?"

Brent laughed, turning his attention from Taryn's bottom to Daniela's top. "Who says science can't be sexy?"

Scowling, Sean walked across the pad and picked up his bottled water, his throat working as he swallowed. Daniela stared after him, wondering why he seemed so affronted. It wasn't as though her breasts were falling out. Taryn was showing a lot more skin.

And yet, Sean was bothered by the idea of Brent filming *her.*

Out of the corner of her eye she watched him take a long drink. Knowing his gaze had been on her, she was intensely aware of the cool morning air against her heated flesh. A bead of sweat dripped down her chest, into the hollow between her breasts.

He slammed the bottle down and she snapped out of her stupor, jerking her attention from Sean to Brent. Of course, he'd caught the moment on film, and captured something far more intimate than a flash of skin.

Perhaps that had been his intention all along.

Brent moved the lens away from her, switching directions with ease. "Tell me why you chose this line of work, Taryn. Sean has a shark story. Jason's friend drowned. Daniela's father was a fisherman, and he used to call her—what was it?"

"Foquita," Sean supplied.

"Yeah. Little seal. Do you have a dolphin story?"

Taryn sat down on a clean section of cement, wiping the sweat off her forehead. "I suppose I do."

By tacit agreement, they all paused to listen. Even Elizabeth.

"I was born in Palos Verdes. Grew up in a house with a private beach."

Jason let out a low whistle. That was some prime real estate.

"My parents traveled a lot, and I was homeschooled. Nannies and tutors. You know how it is."

"No," Brent said wryly. "We don't."

"Well, it wasn't much fun, to be honest. I had everything money could buy, but I didn't care about material things. I hated my huge, empty house and frilly pink room. I wanted to spend all my time at the beach."

"Why?"

"My main caretaker, Ana, was very strict. She was always telling me to do this or that. But she wouldn't go near the water. So I'd swim really far out, where I couldn't hear her. I'd float on my back, pretend to be a mermaid. Stuff like that."

Brent nodded for her to continue.

"I saw dolphins a lot. They play in the surf. I was always trying to catch one to ride it. Of course, I never did." She shrugged, twisting her hands in her lap. "Even so, I considered them my friends. My only friends."

Against her will, Daniela felt a surge of empathy for Taryn. Her own mother had been strict and undemonstrative. As a direct result, Daniela hadn't wanted children. They were such an immense responsibility, and far too easy to let down.

Then she'd gotten pregnant—surprise. She'd never thought maternal instincts would blindside her, but they had. Sean, who rarely got sentimental, had also been caught off-guard by strong feelings during her pregnancy. He was enamored with her curvy body, devoted to her health and comfort, and not-so-secretly proud of their growing baby.

They'd never been closer.

"We're a maudlin bunch," Jason mused, interrupting her thoughts. "I didn't expect it from Taryn."

Daniela hadn't expected it, either, although she'd seen a hint of Taryn's darker side. Maybe her sunny perfection was just a facade.

"What about you, Liz? Surely you have a more uplifting story."

Elizabeth picked up her brush and resumed scrubbing. "I don't have a story. I like birds. That's all."

Brent sharpened his focus on her. "What about birds do you admire?"

She glanced up at the sky. "Their freedom, I guess. Their ease of movement and effortless grace." After a moment, she added, "I'm interested in the behavioral stuff, too. Some birds mate for life. Many species are monogamous, actually."

"Are your parents divorced?"

She gave him a dirty look. "No. And now I'm convinced you're filming a reality show. *Mad Scientists.*"

Brent turned the camera toward Jason. "Your parents still together?"

He smiled at Elizabeth. "Yes."

"Daniela?"

"Yes." Physically, anyway.

"Taryn?"

"No. They're both remarried. And desperately unhappy."

"Sean?"

He shook his head. Daniela knew Sean had taken his parents' divorce hard. He'd once told her that his greatest fear in life was turning out like his father. Angry and bitter and very much alone.

Brent turned off his camera. "Mine are also divorced. That's three against three."

Considering Sean and Daniela's failed marriage, the odds favored divorce. Another depressing topic.

Taking a deep breath, she grabbed her brush and went back to work, scrubbing at the debris in a steady, circular motion. If only she could erase all of the terrible things she'd said and done to Sean the same way.

She'd wash off the painful memories, and start fresh again.

Chapter 10

Daniela made her way along the path to the sea lion blind, her hair whipping around her face.

The wind had kicked up again, stealing every hint of warmth.

Brent offered to accompany her, but Daniela wanted to be alone. She needed some time to think about her reawakened feelings for Sean.

Had she given up on him too soon?

She knew he'd tried harder than she had to make their marriage work. After the accident, he'd given her space. Too much space. And when he started pushing her to get well, to let go of her grief and accept his touch again, she'd…panicked.

Making a sound of frustration, she pushed the hair out of her eyes. It was foolish to rehash the past, but she couldn't help it. The more she thought about Sean, the more confused she became.

She ducked into the blind and closed the door behind her, shutting out the rest of the world. Inside, she was met by silence. There was no wind, no sound, no sunlight. Just a cramped, airless space.

Smothering a surge of anxiety, she picked up a pair of binoculars, examining the shoreline. When she noticed a rash of cormorants circling the air above Dead Man's Beach, her mouth dropped open.

"Well, I'll be damned," she murmured, her heart beating faster.

The wounded seal had been nowhere near Sea Lion Cove yesterday, and Daniela hadn't expected to see hide nor hair of him again. She couldn't see his body on the sand, so she wasn't sure he was there. Hoping the bird formation wasn't just an unhappy coincidence, she set aside the binoculars and searched the shelves for supplies.

After shoving a pair of wire cutters, a can of formula and a few first aid items into a canvas tote bag, she was off, scrambling toward the small beach. It wasn't easy to get to, but Daniela was a fairly good climber. The way back up would pose more of a challenge, but she didn't worry about that as she descended the short cliffs.

In a few moments, she'd maneuvered her way down to the beach. Kneeling behind a large rock, one of the last opportunities for cover, she surveyed the scene.

The wounded seal was there, lying on his side, his breathing labored. The birds who'd plagued him on the other side of the island were keeping their distance, but not because the pup was in better shape than yesterday.

A full-grown Northern elephant seal lounged at the edge of the water, his considerable bulk settled in a rut on the sand. The birds stayed high for good reason. Male elephant seals, called bulls, were loud, toothy and cantankerous.

This one must have weighed at least five thousand pounds.

"Jesus," she whispered, considering her options. Elephant seals rarely attacked humans, but they would charge if they felt threatened. She couldn't outrun an angry bull on sand, and the area was narrow, surrounded by steep rock on three sides. If he made a move on her out in the open, she'd be in big trouble.

But if she didn't act soon, the pup would surely die.

She hesitated, her eyes on the wounded animal. Elephant seals had been known to kill harbor seals. The bull probably considered this beach his personal stomping ground, and could very well trample the unprotected pup.

She waited, hoping the elephant seal would get bored and swim away. The harbor seal turned his head toward her and bleated weakly. The desperate sound tugged on Daniela's heartstrings, and the sight of his liquid brown eyes, so full of pain, strengthened her resolve. She couldn't stand by and watch him suffer a moment longer.

Legs trembling, she removed her jacket and rose from her crouched position. At five-two, her full height didn't impress anyone, especially not the lounging bull. When she moved out from behind the rock, he snuffled into the air, his fleshy nose wobbling with indignation.

While some seals and sea lions were friendly, others were skittish and quick to strike, as fractious as wild dogs. Daniela had a faint scar on her backside to prove it.

Sean had often said it was his favorite place to kiss.

Nevertheless, she wasn't keen on getting bit again. Beneath that bulbous proboscis, an elephant seal had a powerful set of jaws, capable of breaking bones.

Pulse pounding with adrenaline, she edged her way along the base of the cliff behind the tiny beach. If the bull charged, she could try to take cover among the smaller clusters of rocks that jutted from the sand, but there was no safe hiding place, and no real escape, other than the way she came.

She approached the pup warily, keeping her eyes on the bull in the shallow surf. He made a braying sound, warning her to retreat. The gulls and cormorants overhead cawed and circled, wings flapping with excitement.

Farallon Island didn't have the luxury of an emergency medical clinic or round-the-clock veterinary services. On rare occasions, an injured animal was taken to the Marine Mammal Center in San Francisco for care and rehabilitation. In this instance, whatever Daniela could do would have to suffice.

Luckily, the plastic ring didn't appear to be lacerating the pup's flesh, and the seal's temperament was docile. He allowed her to examine him in stoic silence.

Just as she was about to snip the plastic, the bull on the beach let out a thunderous roar.

Frozen with fear, she watched the elephant seal rush toward her, his massive body slamming across the short beach.

Her choices were to drop everything and run, leaving the seal behind, or to attempt to drag the pup to safety. Blood thundering in her ears, she wrapped her arms around his plump middle and heaved backward, her heels seeking purchase in the shifting sand.

She didn't make it. She didn't even come close. The pup was small, less than fifty pounds, and Sean could have picked up two or three of these little guys, but Daniela couldn't even handle one. Before she knew it, she was flat on her butt, staring up at a huge elephant seal, her face just inches from his ugly mug.

He bellowed, misting her cheeks with what had to

have been the most awful halitosis in the entire animal kingdom.

Tears filled her eyes even as the smell soured her stomach. "No," she screamed, hugging the pup closer. "Leave us alone!"

In some part of her mind, she knew she was acting like a madwoman. This wounded seal wasn't her baby. He wasn't a human being. He wasn't even a pet.

And yet, in that moment, she'd have risked her life to protect him. She continued to hold her ground, her chest heaving with pent-up emotion.

For whatever reason, the bull didn't attack. With another disgruntled roar, he turned and loped away, his portly backside disappearing into the crashing surf.

Amazed by the strange sequence of events, and thankful to be unharmed, Daniela let out a ragged laugh. "Well, I ran *him* off, didn't I?" she said, looking down at the speckled pup. Sniffling, she trimmed away the ring around his neck.

His relief was palpable, and instantaneous. He bleated again, as if in thanks.

She poured the can of formula into a stout glass bottle and attached a sturdy rubber nipple. Some animals wouldn't take food this way, but when she poured a few drops into the palm of her hand, he nuzzled her hungrily, and when she put the bottle to his mouth, he sucked the nutrient-rich liquid down in record time.

For Daniela, helping a wounded animal was always satisfying, but her connection to this pup was special. She'd saved him, of that she was sure. And, in some way, he'd saved her. It felt as though a piece of debris had been wrapped around her chest for the past two years, constricting her heart. For the first time in a long while, she could breathe.

Once the young seal's hunger was sated, he drowsed in her arms, exhausted from the life-or-death battle his body had been fighting. Daniela cuddled him closer, crooning softly. She didn't need a therapist to tell her that he reminded her of the child she'd lost.

After some initial anxiety about giving birth and raising a child, she'd settled into the idea of becoming a mother. She'd decided to breast-feed. Sean had teased her about the amount of research she'd done on the subject, saying she was already well-equipped for the job.

A few days after the accident, when her milk came in, she'd wept. Without a baby to nurse, there'd been no easy way to diminish her discomfort, and the swelling had been excruciating. Her breasts had been so full they hurt, and her arms had ached from emptiness.

Pained by the memory, she cradled the chubby little seal against her chest, singing Spanish lullabies and longing for something that could never be.

After a few moments, he roused. His neck was rubbed raw and several peck marks dotted his speckled coat, but he was healthy enough to be set free. Drawn to the lure of the sea, he wriggled away from her, waddling across the sand and sliding into the water with a soft, celebratory splash.

She walked to the shoreline and stared out at the Perfect Wave, feeling the wind lift her hair and caress her overheated face. When she turned back toward the cliffs, she saw Sean leaning against the same rock formation she'd climbed down to get onto the beach. With the sound of the crashing surf, she hadn't heard his approach, so she had no idea how long he'd been watching her. Now the tide was coming in, soaking the sand at her feet.

If she'd tarried here much longer, she'd have been trapped.

Feeling foolish, she gathered up her tote bag and jacket and trudged toward him, anticipating a lecture. But what she saw on his face wasn't reproof. It was grief. He must have seen her cuddling the baby seal, and it was clear he was having the same reaction she had.

His mouth was thin-lipped with anguish and his eyes glittered with unshed tears.

Daniela had only seen Sean cry once, after Natalie's funeral. He'd never been comfortable showing this level of emotion, and she'd often wondered if he were capable of *feeling* it.

Muttering a hoarse curse, he pressed his fingertips to his eyelids, as if he could staunch the flow of tears that way.

She couldn't watch another person suffer without offering her assistance, and this was Sean, the love of her life, so she dropped her things and put her arms around him.

Too often, she'd assumed he didn't understand how she felt. And how could he, when she refused to let him in? Now she was faced with more evidence that she'd been wrong. Maybe he'd been as devastated by the death of their child as she had.

I'd have done anything to take your pain, he'd said, and she knew that was true.

Trying to return the favor, she buried her face in the front of his shirt and held him close, smoothing her hands across his back, stroking the nape of his neck. He wept silently, his shoulders trembling under her fingertips, his arms slipping around her waist. Her heart bled for him, tears burning at her own eyes. At the same time, it felt good to share this moment, and absorb his grief.

Too often, she'd cried alone.

After a few moments, he straightened a little, seeming to recover from the uncharacteristic emotional display.

His flannel shirt was soft against her cheek, and he smelled wonderfully masculine, like clean sweat and warm skin. Without making a conscious choice to do so, she inhaled a deep breath and nuzzled closer, her lips touching his throat.

The muscles in his arms tensed, but he didn't pull away.

She hadn't meant for the embrace to become heated. One of his hands was resting just above her waist, his thumb making lazy circles over her rib cage, close to the underside of her breast.

Daniela glanced up at him cautiously, moistening her lips. His heavy-lidded gaze dropped from her mouth to her breasts, and even if she hadn't seen the arousal in his eyes, she could feel it, swelling against her belly.

A beat pulsed between her legs and the tips of her breasts tingled, aching for his touch.

Sean was a red-blooded man, like any other. There was no denying that he wanted her physically, but she knew he wouldn't take this any further, because of all the times she'd rejected him in the past.

With trembling hands, she reached up to touch his strong, angular face, brushing away the tears. Although he tensed at the contact, she didn't stop. Holding his gaze, she explored the soft bristle of whiskers along his jaw, finding their texture uniquely pleasurable. She wanted to feel the rasp of that stubble all over her body, and the sensation of his hard mouth on hers, so she stood on tiptoe, pressing her lips to his.

For a moment, she thought he wasn't going to respond, but when he did, it was like a dam breaking.

With a groan, he lifted her up, cupping her bottom in his hands and fitting his erection against the apex of her thighs. She gasped, opening her mouth for him, and he thrust his tongue inside, taking everything she offered and then some. It was the least tender, most inelegant kiss he'd ever given her, by far.

Stumbling forward in the sand, he fell on top of her, catching himself with his palms and raining feverish kisses over her jaw, his scruffy chin scraping her face.

He was clumsy, overzealous and totally off-target.

"My mouth is right here," she said helpfully, touching her lips.

"Sorry," he panted, laughing at himself a little before he dove in again. The next attempt was much more successful, but then, he'd always been eager to please. It was his willingness to take direction that made him so damned good in bed, not any technique he'd learned with the women he'd had before her.

This time, he curbed his enthusiasm, finding her mouth with practiced ease and stroking her tongue with his. He also found her breast, cupping the soft weight in his palm and brushing his thumb back and forth over her stiff little nipple.

She moaned, arching into his hand and lifting her hips, encouraging him. He rocked between her legs, rubbing the swollen length of his erection against the cleft of her sex while he kissed and caressed her.

Daniela melted with pleasure.

Then the surf rushed in, wetting her boots.

"Damn!" Sean pushed himself off her, looking down at the soaked knees of his jeans. Clearly intent on continuing what they'd started, he scooped her up and dragged her away from the shore, lowering his mouth to kiss her again.

"Wait," she said, bracing her palms against his chest. She turned her head to the side, trying to catch her breath. The cold splash of reality had brought to mind several reasons why making out on this beach was a bad idea. While they were reenacting *From Here to Eternity,* that territorial bull could come back. "There was an elephant seal."

"What?"

"There was a bull here a few minutes ago. He was kind of, uh…grumpy."

"What!" He scrambled to his feet, his eyes on the shoreline. "Are you *insane?*"

She got up, brushing sand from her clothes. Now she would get a dressing-down, and not the kind she'd been looking forward to.

"You climbed down to an unprotected beach to hang out with a Northern elephant seal? He could have trampled you and the pup!"

Letting out a frustrated breath, she picked up her jacket and her tote bag and started toward the cliffs. Predictably, she had trouble climbing the steep, slippery rocks, which gave Sean another reason to be angry.

"What if you'd been injured?" he asked, boosting her up. "What would you have done when the tide came in?"

"Been swept away, I guess."

His hand lingered on her fanny. "Didn't you learn your lesson about wild animals the last time one bit you in the ass?"

"Apparently not."

Ascending the cliffs required a certain amount of effort and concentration, so Sean stopped scolding in favor of helping her navigate the climb. They'd traversed terrain like this on countless occasions, so he knew her skill level. If he put his hands on her more than was strictly necessary, it was only because she hadn't hiked in a while.

By the time they reached the sea lion blind, they were both breathing hard. Her cheeks were suffused with heat and a fine sheen of perspiration coated her skin. Pretending her response was due to exertion, not arousal, she hazarded another glance at him. "How did you know I was on the beach?"

"I followed the birds."

She nodded, crossing her arms over her chest. "I shouldn't have gone down there alone. You're right. It was…unsafe."

He massaged his forehead, a gesture she knew he used when he was trying to focus. "I don't like to see you take unnecessary risks."

"You tag sharks for a living," she felt compelled to mention.

"I think you should go back to San Diego."

Her temper bubbled up, hot and bright. He thought she should leave because of what happened *after* the elephant seal encounter, not before. "Why don't you want me here?" she asked, getting closer to him. "Am I making you uncomfortable?"

His gaze dragged along the inner curves of her breasts, as tangible as a caress. "You know damned well you're making me uncomfortable."

"Maybe you should do something about it."

An emotion she couldn't identify crossed over his features. She'd never been this suggestive, but she'd never had to be. In their relationship, he'd made all the first moves. "No," he said in a cold voice, cutting her dead.

Her mouth dropped open. She could feel heat coming off him in waves, but instead of kissing her senseless, he was turning her down. "Why?"

He looked away, refusing to answer.

"Why?" she repeated, her stomach churning with dread.

"Because you broke my *heart*," he bit out, thrusting a

hand through his hair. "Jesus, Dani, why do you think? Being near you hurts like hell. Touching you makes me lose my mind. I can't even look at you without dying inside."

Daniela stared at him in wonder, feeling her chest tighten and her throat close up. She felt exactly the same way he did. "You broke my heart, too," she whispered, hugging her arms around herself. "You're the one who filed for divorce."

He studied her for a long moment, his mouth grim. "I said I would, the day you told me to leave. Remember?"

She nodded, feeling miserable.

"Why did you sign the divorce papers?" he asked.

"I—I thought you wanted to get on with your life."

"I did. I still do."

Tears of despair flooded her eyes. Of course he did. She was too difficult, too fractured, too complicated.

It was too hard to be with her, so he'd given up and moved on.

She was too late.

"I'm sorry," he said quietly.

She gave him a brittle smile. "I'm sorry, too."

Turning away from him, she shrugged into her jacket and walked out the door, brushing the tears from her eyes.

She wasn't sure why she was so disappointed, or what she'd expected. And she couldn't bear to analyze her wanton behavior. If she wanted a sexual fling, she could approach Jason, or any other man. With Sean, there would always be strings attached.

Besides, she hadn't come here to reconcile an impossibly damaged relationship. The two of them could become friends and colleagues again, not partners.

Not lovers.

Her emotional breakdown had killed their marriage. She'd driven him away, and never made one single attempt at reconciliation. She couldn't give him what he needed—a happy family—and he didn't deserve anything less.

Taking a deep breath, Daniela looked up at the bleak, bright sky, wishing things had played out differently.

Sometimes, life's cards were too hard to hold.

Chapter 11

Sean wanted to kick himself.

On the way to the house, he stared at the back of Daniela's head, trying to ignore the assault on his senses and the ache in his groin. His hands were shaking with need, so he shoved them into his pockets, wishing he didn't remember all the ways he'd touched her over the course of their marriage. God, he'd been a sex maniac. Even while she was pregnant, he was constantly at her. Had he been too demanding? Too rough, too insatiable?

He stifled a groan, cursing himself in silence. The long stint of abstinence had almost shattered his self-control. On Dead Man's Beach, he'd fallen on her like a raving lunatic. In the sea lion blind, he'd wanted to take her to the floor, tear her clothes off and bury himself in her. She'd have let him, too.

Damn. Why hadn't he just gone ahead and done it?

During the last year of their marriage, he'd have given

anything for a chance to have her in his arms again. He'd fantasized about making love to her, his own wife, constantly. She'd needed space, but he'd needed *her.*

Countless times, he'd imagined her brushing her lips over his. Threading her fingers through his hair and pulling his mouth down to hers. Whispering her most intimate desires in his ear, begging him to make her feel good again.

He'd been desperate to give her pleasure, to fill up the empty places inside her, to kiss the hurt away. She'd never allowed him to.

And now…it wasn't enough. Indulging in a physical relationship with Daniela, at this point, was a recipe for disaster. He'd never get over her that way. One kiss, and he'd been ready to declare his undying affection and ravage her in the sand.

He was weak where she was concerned, but he wasn't stupid. Seeing her again had brought back a lot of old memories. Although their marriage hadn't been perfect, it had been damned good. He'd been crazy about her, and it was hard to let her go. Being thrown together in cramped quarters, it was only natural for him to feel…nostalgic.

He'd loved her so much.

After the accident, when he found out she was going to be okay, he'd been overwhelmed with relief. He remembered sitting by her bedside, getting choked up just looking at her. Hours upon hours had passed, while he'd done nothing but watch her sleep.

The day she'd come home from the hospital, he'd been an emotional wreck. Maybe he'd smothered her with attention, or hovered too much. He'd been so happy she was alive. Every moment he'd spent with her seemed like a gift—one she'd actively rejected.

No matter how many times he tried to reconnect

with her, she'd refused to let him in. He'd attempted to engage her in a thousand different ways. She'd remained unapproachable, untouchable, unresponsive. Lost to him.

His love hadn't been enough for her then. And her body wasn't enough for him now.

It wasn't easy to deny her, but it was easier than letting his guard down. Her emotional withdrawal, and their subsequent divorce, had devastated him. He'd rather feel nothing than experience that kind of pain again.

As they came closer to the landing, late afternoon fog rolled in from the Pacific, settling over the island like a shroud. The creepy old Victorian seemed to rise out of the mist. A few hundred yards beyond the shore, smoke curled from the mouth of Skull Rock.

Earlier, he and Jason had discussed their concerns about the ruined engine. Although it seemed far-fetched, they had to consider the possibility that an intruder had set foot on the island. "Promise me you won't wander off alone again," he said to Daniela. "It isn't safe here, considering what happened yesterday."

Her brows drew together. "What do you mean?"

"Jason thinks the engine may have been sabotaged."

"By whom? The seal-skinner?"

He sighed, shaking his head. "The cage-divers have a Zodiac, and we've had some run-ins with them in the past."

"About chumming?"

"Yeah. I asked them to stop. They told me to piss off."

She cast him a chiding glance. "I suppose you said a polite goodbye after that."

Actually, he'd called the crew leader an asshole, when push had come to shove. "I was at least as polite as they were," he muttered. "Until we find out what went wrong, you shouldn't wander off alone. Neither should Taryn or Elizabeth."

"What about you and the other men?"

"We can defend ourselves."

Her eyes wandered across his torso, and a tiny crease appeared between her brows. Before they got married, he'd given her a couple of lessons in self-defense. Small, feminine and beautiful, she was an ideal target for a predator.

Maybe she was thinking about kneeing him in the groin, one of the moves he'd taught her, because her gaze dropped to the fly of his jeans. Or maybe she was recalling his inappropriate arousal during one of those demonstrations, which had devolved into a playful wrestling match and steamy sex on the floor.

She looked away, a faint blush tingeing her cheeks. "Fine," she said. "I won't go anywhere alone."

Her acquiescence wasn't much of a victory, and he didn't feel any better for having it. He needed a cold shower and a hot meal, in that order, but he knew he wouldn't be satisfied with those things, either. It was Daniela's turn to cook. Eating with her used to be a sensual experience. Now, he'd probably choke on his regrets.

He couldn't wait to get off this miserable island. Being here with her was like descending into a new level of hell.

Before going in, she took him by the hand, surprising him. "I just need to tell you…I was wrong. Everything that happened was my fault. I'm sorry I pushed you away." Her eyes searched his for a moment, cutting straight to the heart.

He wanted to say she was mistaken, that his inability to console her had been far more detrimental to their relationship, but the words stuck in his throat. While he faltered, trying to pull himself together, she disappeared inside the house.

Several long, arduous moments passed before he was able to follow.

Daniela was tired of crying.

She cracked a couple of eggs into a bowl with more force than was necessary, mixing the ingredients with shaking hands.

There were too many conflicting feelings to sort through, too many confusing thoughts and words and images. No matter what Sean said, she knew he wanted her, and her body throbbed in response to his arousal.

Maybe it was hopeless, and they were destined to be apart. She couldn't figure it out right now. Instead of trying, she worked her fingers into the tamale dough, squeezing it into submission. Pounding its flat, expressionless face.

"Pretending that's Sean?"

She looked from the ceramic bowl to Jason's knowing smile. "Why would I do that?" she asked, blowing the bangs off her forehead.

"Because he deserves it."

"For what?"

He held her gaze. "Being such a fool as to lose you."

Daniela frowned, wondering why he was flirting with her when he was clearly interested in another woman. "You have a problem," she decided, returning her attention to kneading.

"I know," he said with a heavy sigh.

"Elizabeth won't go for you if your attention wanders easily."

"That does present a challenge," he agreed.

"Why do you do it?"

"Do what?"

"Let your eye rove."

He paused, considering. "I guess I'm looking for something I haven't found yet. Or maybe I just have a short attention span." His mouth twisted with dissatisfaction, as if he didn't like that about himself. "Did Sean's eye never rove?"

"His eye? Yes." Like most men, Sean had noticed other women. Before the accident, it hadn't bothered her. "He might have looked, but he didn't *linger*."

"Hmm."

"You linger."

"Lingering is much more fun."

It was her turn to laugh. "Are you going to help me make these tamales, or keep trying to have your wicked way with me?"

"You aren't even tempted. I must be losing my touch."

"I don't think so."

His gaze darkened. "Now you're encouraging me."

"If I did, you'd get bored."

"I doubt it."

Daniela smiled, thinking Elizabeth would have some stiff competition if she wasn't so hung up on Sean. "Have you ever wrapped corn husks?"

"No. We use banana leaves on the islands."

"Same idea," she said, placing a small amount of dough in the center of an unwrapped husk, demonstrating the technique. After adding the meat filling, she closed the edges of the husk and tied it up into a neat little package.

Jason watched carefully, mimicking her movements. He was a very quick study.

They continued making tamales together, falling into an easy rhythm. She had no siblings and few close friends, most of whom she'd alienated over the past two years. The only person she communicated with on a regular basis was

Mamá, who meant well but failed to provide unconditional support.

When the tamales were finished steaming, she brought them out to the living room, along with a pitcher of juice and a large platter of mixed vegetables and rice. Jason had beer with his meal, but Sean wasn't drinking. He'd been tense since he came downstairs, watching her put food on the table in quiet contemplation.

"So what's up with the engine?" Brent asked, taking a seat next to Sean. "Seems kind of weird that the oars were missing."

"Yes," Jason said, glancing at Daniela. "It does. I can't rule out the possibility that it was tampered with."

Brent's brows rose. "You think someone came onto the island again?"

"Maybe. We've had some static from the guys who run the cage-diving operation. Last season, they tried a new kind of chum, some noxious mixture with blood meal and tuna parts. The whole island reeked like fish ass."

Taryn wrinkled her nose, as if remembering the smell. "Jason went out to talk to them about it, and the discussion almost came to blows."

"Bastards," he said, taking another bite. "They'd rather fight than talk. Sean exchanged some strong words with them the season before, too."

Brent arched a brow. "Strong words, from Sean?"

"They started it," he muttered.

"Do you think they hold a grudge?"

"It's possible."

"How would they access the island?"

Jason swallowed a mouthful of rice before he spoke. "They have an inflatable boat."

"The cage-divers come on weekends," Elizabeth pointed out. "Today's Friday."

"Right," Jason said. "I think we should use the buddy system from now on. Stay in radio contact, and don't go off alone."

Elizabeth bristled. "I'm the only ornithologist. It doesn't make any sense for anyone to hang out with me at the bird blind."

"I'd be happy to escort you," Jason said.

She narrowed her eyes at him. "For what purpose? I seriously doubt that anyone has been sneaking around on the island."

"Who do you think sabotaged the engine, if not them?" Brent asked.

Elizabeth pushed aside her plate. Her face was pale and serious. "Maybe you did."

His jaw went slack. "Why would I do it?"

"For your stupid documentary," she said in a scathing tone. "You probably skinned the seal to create drama. And you'd sell your soul for some shark attack footage."

The tension in the room skyrocketed. Elizabeth's accusation was wild, and insulting—but was it off base?

"No," Brent said quietly. "I wouldn't hurt an animal, and I'd never use footage like that in my work. Not for any price. You, of all people, should know that."

Her mouth thinned. "I have no idea what you're talking about."

"As you wish," he murmured.

Jason crossed his arms over his chest. "Spill it."

"It's not my story to tell," Brent said.

Elizabeth leaped to her feet, the legs of her chair scraping across the hardwood floor. "There is no story."

When she hurried toward the door, Jason caught up with her in three easy strides. "Like hell there isn't," he said, grabbing her wrist.

Gasping, she drew back her other arm and slapped him across the face. The sound was like the crack of a whip.

Jason released her arm abruptly. The mark of her hand stood out on his dark cheek.

"I'm sorry," she sputtered, horrified. Before he could react to the blow, she spun away from him and ran out the door.

Stunned, Jason touched the side of his face.

"I'll go after her," Taryn said, rising.

Daniela stood also. "Me, too."

"Hang on," Sean said, striding toward the door. It was pitch black outside. He looked from Jason to Brent, a muscle in his jaw ticking. "I don't give a damn whose story it is. If there's something we need to know, tell us."

"Fine," Brent said, defeated. "It's not that important. Ancient history, really. Let the girls go."

Taryn pulled her jacket off the hook and put it on. Daniela rushed to do the same. Sean probably didn't want them to follow Elizabeth anywhere, but she shouldn't be alone on the cliffs at night, under any circumstances.

"Take the flashlight," Sean said, handing it to Daniela. "And be careful."

She donned her wool cap. "Of course. A bit of girl talk and everything will be fine."

Although he looked as though he wanted to come along, he didn't press the issue. Elizabeth would be more comfortable with other women. After one last glance at Sean, Daniela walked out the door, and Taryn pulled it shut behind them.

"Don't turn on the light yet," Taryn said, studying the landscape. Most of the fog had cleared and a waning moon was out, barely visible through wispy layers of clouds. "There." Taryn pointed at the path to the tower.

Elizabeth's gray windbreaker appeared almost white in the moonlight, an ethereal shape ascending the cliff.

"She *would* go that direction," Daniela muttered. Shouting at her to come back was pointless; their voices would be carried away on the wind. They started walking, turning on the flashlight to illuminate their footsteps.

At night, the pebble-strewn path was twice as dangerous. With painstaking care they made their way up the cliff. Finally, they reached the summit. Elizabeth was standing at the edge of the lighthouse tower, contemplating the pounding surf and jagged cliffs below.

She and Taryn exchanged a worried glance. Daniela didn't want to startle Elizabeth, who was dangerously close to a sharp drop-off.

"My father committed suicide," she said, looking over her shoulder. "Brent filmed it."

Daniela sucked in a sharp breath.

"Well, he filmed part of it. He didn't actually die that time. No, he hung on for years and years, bragging about how he'd cheated death." She let out a harsh laugh, shaking her head. "He'd cheated death."

Taryn frowned at her cryptic words. "What do you mean?"

"He was a shark enthusiast. A thrill seeker. He ran adventure tours in Daytona Beach. People would pay to watch him swim with sharks."

Daniela's jaw dropped.

"About fifteen years ago, Brent went on one of his tours. He must have been around eighteen at the time. He filmed the attack."

"Oh my God," Taryn murmured.

"My father considered that his shining moment," she said, raising one fist in a mocking salutation. "He'd survived a shark attack! And he wanted to revel in that dubious glory. But Brent wouldn't release the footage."

Daniela inched closer.

"Brent stood by while my father risked his life, and continued filming while the shark took his legs."

"He couldn't have helped," Taryn said. "We all know it's too dangerous to enter the water during an attack."

"He shouldn't have been filming at all!"

"Maybe not," Taryn said. "But that was a long time ago. Don't you think he made the right decision, about not releasing the footage? It's not fair to accuse him of wrong-doing now, because of a past mistake."

Daniela was surprised by Taryn's calm assurance. It was exactly what Elizabeth needed. Reason, rather than comfort. "I agree," Daniela said, putting her hand on Elizabeth's shoulder. "You should talk to him about it. Work things out."

Elizabeth flinched, but she didn't wrench away. "There's nothing to work out. We don't have to be friends."

"Did you know he would be here?" Daniela asked.

"Of course. I thought we could be civil, on the off chance that he recognized me."

"That wasn't exactly civil," Taryn said.

After a significant pause, Elizabeth nodded. "You're right. I owe him an apology." With a small grimace, she shook her head. "I'll have to apologize to Jason, too. And he's already so damned smug."

Daniela wanted to continue the conversation, and make sure Elizabeth was really okay, but a light rain began to fall, stinging her cheeks.

"Let's go in before the path gets slippery," Taryn recommended.

Hoping the issue would soon be resolved, Daniela started down the path, Taryn and Elizabeth following close behind. She'd feel more relieved once they were inside. The temperature had dropped and the wind had picked up, cutting through her light jacket. Her hands and face were ice cold.

As they rounded the steepest corner, approaching the sheer drop-off into the whirlpool below, she heard a surprised cry behind her.

Taryn stumbled forward, crashing into her back. The flashlight fell from her hands, and Daniela went sprawling, hurtling toward the safety rail. Although she expected a painful impact, the railing gave way with sickening ease.

She experienced a moment of weightlessness, and the bizarre sensation of tumbling through space. She screamed, her arms and legs flailing.

The only thing she hit was water.

Chapter 12

The drop from the cliff to the water was less than twenty feet, but the impact was like a punch to the stomach. The shock of the blow immobilized her and the cold robbed her breath.

She plummeted deep underwater, surrounded by a black abyss.

As soon as she stopped sinking, Daniela began to kick frantically, clawing her way back to the surface. But she was hampered by her wet clothing. The pockets of her jacket had filled with water and her boots felt like sandbags. Taking them off wasn't an option, because they protected her from the cold, and her first priority was getting air.

She fought hard, all the way to the top, and broke through at long last, opening her mouth to gasp. But her lungs refused to expand. Her body felt numb. A powerful wave crashed over her head, covering her in icy darkness.

Disconnectedly, she wondered how long it would take to drown.

Pinpricks of light flashed behind her eyelids and the cold seeped in, permeating the layers of her clothing and chilling her to the bone. If she didn't get some oxygen on her next try, she would die.

And she'd only been in the water a few seconds.

Refusing to give up, she pumped her legs again, moving her arms in frantic paddling motions. The cold had seized her lungs. She felt disembodied, disoriented. Like she was swimming in slush.

Panicking, she let out a silent scream, struggling her way back up to the surface. This time, when she broke through, she was able to fill her lungs with fresh, clean air. She treaded water frantically, gasping for help.

On the cliffs above her, Elizabeth was calling her name, pointing the beam of the flashlight in her direction.

Another wave surged up, splashing her face. Daniela choked and sputtered, tasting salt. "Sean!" she yelled, her voice hoarse with emotion. Never mind that he wasn't within hearing range; his was the name that leaped to her lips.

"Hang on, Daniela," Elizabeth called out. "Taryn ran to get help. Stay with me!"

Powerful currents tugged her every which way, smashing her into the rocks, scraping her along the jagged edges. Swimming against the flow was impossible, and there was nowhere to haul herself out. She needed to get a grip on something, anything. And she had to do it quick, because she couldn't keep her head above water much longer. Already, her muscles were like jelly.

"There," Elizabeth shouted, shining the beam of light on a section of wet, slippery rock. "Grab on right there, Daniela!"

The surface was perforated with holes, large and small. With her last ounce of strength, Daniela swam for it, straining toward the light. A wave brought her the last few feet, slamming her face so hard she saw stars.

Grimacing, she found a handhold in the rock and clung to it, hanging on for dear life.

Time went by and her arms lost their feeling. She lost count of the number of waves that washed over her. Fear of sharks kept her there, gripping the slippery rocks. It wasn't as though they were sleeping right now, taking a break from hunting. If she let go and was swept out into the open water, she would be eaten alive.

"Sean," she whispered, pressing her cheek to the wet rock, as if its chiseled surface were his stubbled jaw.

"Daniela!"

It was him; she knew it was him. But her eyelids were too heavy to lift, her limbs too weak to hold her up.

Something soft and rubbery hit the back of her head, rousing her.

"Grab the ring," he ordered. "Damn it, Daniela! Grab the ring or I'm going to come in after you."

She opened her eyes with a low moan, looking behind her. There was a U-shaped flotation device on a heavy white rope, ready to pull her to safety. If she could pry her hands off the rock, she would reach for it. But her arms trembled in protest, refusing to cooperate.

"Grab the ring, Daniela. Do it now!"

In a far corner of her mind, she knew he couldn't come in after her. Although he was an excellent swimmer, the situation was far too dangerous. She doubted he'd be able to grab her, and he'd have just as much trouble getting out afterward. His weight would be twice as difficult for the others to handle on the safety pull.

Her own death seemed like a vague notion, frightening

but fuzzy. The idea of Sean drowning for her, splitting his head open on the jagged rocks…

She let go with one hand, her arm stretching out, numb fingers seeking the rubber ring. The next wave washed her away from the rock, but she managed to hook her arm through the safety ring. Rather than relying on her feeble grip, she tugged the lifesaver over her head, securing it under both arms.

The task was Herculean, and her body paid the price for the effort. Before they'd even started pulling her up, another wave swept in, taking her to oblivion.

Sean thought the night of Daniela's car accident had been the most harrowing of his life. He was wrong. Two years ago, he'd been trapped at Southeast Farallon while she lay in the hospital, close to death. He'd gone out of his mind, worrying about her.

This was worse.

Right now he could *see* her dying, and he felt twice as wretched.

"She's unconscious," he said through clenched teeth. Pulling her up the cliff was a tricky job, fraught with danger. At any moment, she could slip through the ring and tumble back into the water. Her life was hanging by a thread.

And he was holding that thread in his hands.

"She'll be fine," Jason panted. Although Sean was taking most of the weight, Jason was in the second position, which also required a considerable amount of strength. Either of them could lift Daniela up and throw her over their shoulder with ease, but hauling more than a hundred pounds by rope was more difficult.

Precious seconds ticked by.

Her head lolled back and forth, insensible.

Finally, she was within reach. Sean heaved her up the last few feet, adrenaline fueling his movements. He dragged her lifeless body across the ground and stretched her out, flat on her back, along a safer section of path.

Her face was ashen and her lips were blue. "Breathe," he commanded, pressing his lips to hers and filling her lungs with oxygen. "Breathe!"

She sputtered, water gurgling from her mouth. Sean turned her on her side, cradling her head in his lap while she retched and retched. Joyous shouts rang out along the cliff side. Hands patted his back as tears of relief ran down his face.

"Thank God," he murmured, holding her close as she began to shudder uncontrollably. Her skin was like ice. She wasn't out of the woods yet.

Sweeping her into his arms, he made his way down the path, her small body shaking, her wet clothes soaking his. "Make her a hot drink," he snarled as soon as they came in the door. "I'm going to warm her up."

Upstairs, he kicked open the door to the bedroom he shared with Jason, putting her in the only chair. She shivered while he took off her jacket and pulled her top over her head. He knelt to unlace her boots, cursing when the wet laces failed to budge. Taking the knife off his belt, he cut them away.

After getting rid of her boots and socks, he stood her up to strip her pants off. Her panties came down with them, leaving her clad in only a soaked-through bra. The dark circles of her nipples were clearly visible through the transparent fabric. He fumbled with the clasp at her back, trying to ignore the most beautiful breasts in the world when they tumbled free. His towel was hanging on a hook by the door. With trembling hands, he grabbed it, rubbing the terry cloth over her wet hair and pale skin, drying her as best he could.

He unzipped his sleeping bag and put her inside, covering her before he went to work on his own clothes. In less than a minute, he was naked but for a pair of boxer briefs. He kept them on, assuming she'd prefer to have at least one barrier between them.

Jason knocked on the door and stuck his head inside. "This is just hot water," he said, handing Sean a mug. "The tea is still brewing."

"Thanks," he said, taking the mug from Jason and shutting the door behind him. He knelt beside the bed, helping her raise her head to take a sip.

When she'd had enough, he set the mug down and climbed into the sleeping bag with her. Her skin was cold, too cold. Concern for her kept his thoughts pure. Focusing only on getting her warm, he wrapped his arms around her and put his mouth close to hers.

"Breathe in when I exhale," he said. Hypothermia affected the lungs, so filling them with warm air was essential.

Her lips brushed over his as she nodded.

He breathed into her, again and again, giving his heat, his warmth, his life to her. His blood was still pumping with adrenaline, his heart hammering against hers. By slow increments, her skin took on the same temperature as his. His fear and anxiety faded as her trembling subsided. After a while, the tight space inside the sleeping bag wasn't just warm.

It was hot.

Sean buried his face in the hollow of her neck, collapsing with relief. If worry for her had prevented him from responding to the unintentional eroticism of the situation, his relaxing concern had the opposite effect. Her body was so soft, so luscious. He loved every solitary inch of her, not just her breasts. Her belly button was the sexiest thing he'd ever seen. The curve of her spine drove him crazy.

Even the sight of her bare toes turned him on.

He shifted his weight to one side, hoping she wouldn't notice the way his body was reacting to hers. "What happened?"

She moistened her lips. "I don't know."

"Taryn said you fell."

"I—I guess I did. But—" She broke off, frowning.

"What?"

"I felt something hit me."

He froze. "Hit you where?"

"In the back."

"Like a push?"

She gave him a strange look. "No. More like a bump. Like Taryn lost her balance and bumped into me."

His stomach clenched with dread.

"I thought the safety rail would stop my forward momentum, but it didn't. When I hit the side of the railing, it just…fell away."

"That's strange," he said. "I checked the rail earlier this week. It was solid."

Daniela stared up at him, her eyes dark and deep in the lamplight. "I don't know what to say. Maybe I imagined it." She tore her gaze from his, making a harsh sound. "We all know I'm a little crazy."

"No," he said, feeling his resolve slip. She must have felt it, too, because she glanced his way again, studying his mouth in a way that could have roused a dead man.

Sean wasn't dead. He'd been halfway there, emotionally, much of the time they'd spent apart, but he was alive now. Every fiber of his being was on full alert, every nerve in his body vibrating, every muscle taut.

Any blood that was left in his head rushed south, hardening his erection to a painful degree, and he knew damned well she could feel *that*. Her eyelids got heavy and her mouth went soft. A bead of sweat trickled down his spine, into the waistband of his shorts.

Jason opened the door again. "Tea?"

Sean couldn't take his eyes off Daniela.

"I guess you don't need it," he said, a smirk in his voice.

"Go away," Sean said hoarsely. "Before I kill you."

As soon as Jason closed the door, Daniela threaded her fingers through his hair and lifted her parted lips to his. Making a strangled sound, he gave her what she wanted, thrusting his tongue inside her mouth, tasting her deeply. She moaned, kissing him back with sultry enthusiasm. When he slid his thigh between her legs, pressing hard, she gasped, digging her fingernails into his sweat-slicked back.

He wanted to take her hips in his hands and grind himself against her, stroke his erection along her sweet, hot cleft. He wanted to be inside her.

Panting, he broke contact with her mouth, trying to recover his wits. God, he felt as coarse as a schoolboy. He was going to climax all over her stomach.

"Don't stop," she whispered, her hand drifting down his belly.

He caught her before she went too far. "If you touch me, I'll come."

She nibbled on her lower lip, clearly not put off by the idea. He kissed her again, distracting her, and shifted his thigh from between her legs, making room for his hand. The feel of her wet heat against his fingertips was like heaven. He slid his index finger along the seam of her sex and slipped it inside, where she grasped him snugly.

"God," he muttered, clenching his teeth. "You're so hot."

She squirmed and spread her legs wider, begging him for more. She'd always been responsive, but this display of sensuality was so overt, he almost couldn't hold himself in check. Her scent filled his nostrils as he stroked her, plunging his fingers in and out. Her breasts quivered, the dusky tips jutting forward. His mouth watered to taste her. When she whimpered, he pressed the ball of his thumb to her swollen clit.

That was all it took. One little nudge. She bit her lip to keep from crying out as she shattered, convulsing around his fingers.

If he moved, he'd follow her, so he stayed right where he was, his eyes on her face and his hand between her legs. When she relaxed, blinking up at him as though she'd just drifted back down to earth, he eased back slowly.

His fingers were slick and fragrant with her. He stared at her glistening sex, caught between exquisite pleasure and acute agony, his cock as stiff as Skull Rock. Aware that he was no longer capable of telling her no, she pushed down the front of his shorts. Watching his face, she ran her fingertip down his rigid length.

And that was all it took for him. One simple touch.

Making a soft O with her lips, she wrapped her fingers around him, squeezing and stroking his shaft. When she swept her thumb over the blunt tip, spreading a bead of moisture, he groaned, his body jerking uncontrollably.

She bent her head, touching her tongue to him.

The moment her hot mouth closed around him, he started to climax. She stayed right where she was, drawing him deep.

When it was over, she rested her cheek on his belly, eyes closed.

He wasn't sure how long it took him to recover. Seconds ticked by and silence stretched between them, punctuated only by his thundering heartbeat and ragged breaths. Fighting against post-orgasmic lassitude, and the deeper, more disturbing need to hold her in his arms all night long, he forced himself to roll away.

Still reeling from the encounter, he sat at the edge of the bed. With trembling hands, he pulled his briefs back into place. Their sex life had always been inspired, and he prided himself on having a certain amount of stamina. He'd never gone off at the drop of a hat. Then again, he hadn't had a two-year stint of abstinence since losing his virginity at the tender age of fifteen.

She came up behind him, placing one hand on his shoulder and touching her lips to the center of his back. After what passed between them this afternoon at Dead Man's Beach, not to mention her near-drowning this evening, all of his emotions were on edge. He lurched up from the bed, feeling the hot sting of tears in his eyes once again.

Sean was glad Daniela was letting go of her grief and working through her aversion to touch. Really. And he understood why she felt safe with him, her former husband. But he just couldn't do this with her, not on a purely physical level.

He dug through his belongings, taking out a fresh set of clothes. After changing into them, he tossed her a pair of sweatpants and a T-shirt. While she got dressed, he gathered all of their wet clothes, including her lacy panties, and shoved them in his laundry bag, as if getting rid of the evidence.

Only then did he summon the nerve to look at her.

She was sitting on the lower bunk, arms crossed over her chest, her petite body swimming in his extra-large clothes.

The legs of his sweatpants covered her feet and then some, and the short sleeves of his T-shirt hung down past her elbows.

Her big brown eyes seemed to take up half her face.

There was a scrape on her cheekbone that would probably look worse tomorrow, and another, smaller mark on her chin. He hadn't really noticed them until now, and that made him feel like a prize bastard.

She was hurt, and vulnerable; he shouldn't have touched her.

Clenching his jaw, he grabbed a bottle of Tylenol from his pack. Shaking a couple of pills into his palm, he handed them to her, along with the cooling water.

She took the painkillers without complaint.

"I'm going to check the railing," he said. "Do you need anything?"

Raising a trembling hand to her hair, which was drying in wild tangles around her face, she said, "I'd like a warm bath, actually."

Nodding, he left the room, walking down the hall and into the bathroom. He checked the tub to make sure it was clean before he plugged the drain and turned on the faucet. The water ran clear and hot, luckily.

Not asking her permission, he picked her up and carried her to the bathroom, shutting the door behind them.

She allowed him to help her out of his clothes, shivering a little.

"Stay in here until I get back."

Naked, she slipped into the warm water.

Sean didn't mean to look. He certainly didn't mean to look so long, memorizing every dip and curve of a body he'd never stopped fantasizing about. He didn't mean to clench his hands into fists, or make a sound of quiet desperation.

She rested her head against the tub and closed her eyes, biting down on her lush lower lip.

He knew what she was remembering. More than once, he'd begged her to touch herself while he watched. Usually, she laughed off his requests, chiding him softly. But, on one memorable occasion, she'd pulled herself up out of the bubble bath, soapsuds clinging to her gorgeous body, and done exactly what he'd asked.

"I'm going to check the railing," he said, hoarse.

"You mentioned that already."

"Right." Clearing his throat, he left the bathroom.

Downstairs, everyone seemed to be immersed in their own projects, as usual. Brent was editing the day's footage, and Jason was writing an accident report. Elizabeth must have gone to her room, but Taryn was sitting at the table, in front of her laptop.

"Is Daniela okay?" she asked.

His blood, which had only just cooled, began to boil again. The thought of Taryn pushing Daniela filled him with an almost insupportable rage. "She's fine now," he said in a mild tone. "Come into the kitchen for a second."

With a small frown, she closed her laptop and rose from her chair. Jason gave him an assessing look, but he didn't interfere.

The instant Taryn stepped into the kitchen Sean trapped her against the pantry door, putting his face close to hers. "If you ever touch Daniela again," he said in a low, dangerous voice, "I will drag you outside and throw you to the sharks myself!"

She winced, trying to sidestep him. He wouldn't let her. "Elizabeth lost her balance," she said through clenched teeth. "She fell forward, into my back, and I went flying into Daniela. It was an accident."

Sean eased up on her. "Elizabeth hit you first?"

She broke away from him, her eyes flashing with anger. "Yes. If I was going to push anyone off a cliff, it would be you, you stupid jerk."

Sean moved back a step, rubbing a hand over his face. He took a few calming breaths, trying to regain some sense of self-control. "I'm sorry," he said quietly, regretting his actions. "I didn't mean to hurt you."

"Whatever," she said, crossing her arms over her chest.

His fear for Daniela hadn't abated, and he was still curious about the push. Walking out of the kitchen, he glanced upstairs. When pressed, Brent had revealed the story about Elizabeth's father, a struggling tour guide who'd come to a bad end. Sean didn't think Elizabeth had any reason to attack Daniela, however.

"Don't even think about it," Jason warned. "I'm going to talk to Elizabeth myself, and employ a bit more finesse."

"Finesse? Seems like that tactic earned you a slap earlier."

His eyes darkened. "Mind your own business. Taryn said it was an accident, and Elizabeth apologized repeatedly while you were *busy*."

Sean struggled against the urge to grab Jason by the front of the shirt and haul him outside to knock some sense into him. He wasn't taking this situation seriously enough. "Daniela said the railing was loose."

Jason straightened. "Really? It felt fine yesterday."

"I'm going up to the tower to check it."

Brent picked up his camera. "I'll go, too."

"No," Jason said, setting his paperwork aside. "You stay here with the girls. I want to look at it myself."

Although Brent seemed disappointed, he agreed. He was probably upset that he hadn't caught Dani's near-drowning on tape.

Sean and Jason put on their jackets, stepping out into the stormy night. A hard rain had begun to fall, pelting their hoods and shoulders. He hoped it wouldn't wash away evidence that the railing had been loosened by human hands.

They ascended the hill quickly. Near the summit, there was a rash of muddy footprints, left during Daniela's harrowing rescue. Sean bypassed that area, still shaken by the images of her lifeless body, the feel of her chilled skin.

A few feet up the path, the safety railing was hanging at an odd angle, swinging out over the precipice. The base of one post was splintered. When Sean knelt at the footing and righted the post, it stayed in place.

To the average passerby, it looked solid. And yet, the barest touch would topple it again.

While he was down there, he inspected the muddy earth, running his hands over its wet, pebbled surface. There were many small rocks, as always. Loosened by the rain, they made the path even more dangerous.

Sean stood, shaking his head. The post could have splintered when Daniela hit the railing. There was no clean cut in the wood, no definitive evidence of foul play. But together with the boating incident, it was an odd coincidence.

Sean and Jason made their way down the path in grave silence.

"I'm going to call the Coast Guard," Jason said when they arrived at the base of the hill. "Is your cell phone working?"

He took it out of his pocket and turned on the screen. No bars. "I never get service in weather like this."

"Me, either. I'll call from inside."

"They won't send anyone tonight," Sean predicted.

"No. Maybe tomorrow, weather permitting."

Sean contemplated the howling wind and hammering rain, and doubted it.

"I'll sleep downstairs," Jason added. "Nobody's getting through the front door on my watch."

It wasn't a bad idea. But what if the threat was already inside?

Sean had to consider the possibility that one of his colleagues was responsible. Now that he'd calmed down, he couldn't believe Taryn was a coldhearted murderess. Elizabeth seemed prickly, not psychotic. And Brent was just a starving artist. If he wanted to collect shark attack footage, he'd have better odds with a daring group of divers.

"I'll talk to Elizabeth tonight," Jason said, his expression stark. "Tomorrow, we can take turns snooping around. Check the rooms."

Sean nodded. At this point, he didn't trust anyone—not even Jason. The only person he felt comfortable with was Daniela, and he wasn't going to leave her side until she was safe and secure, back on the mainland.

Chapter 13

Daniela stayed in the bath until the water cooled. Although she was exhausted, her mind refused to relax.

For months after the accident, she'd refused Sean's touch. She hadn't been with anyone since the divorce, either. She hadn't felt like it.

In the past year, her needs had changed. Ironically, she'd missed Sean. She'd been somewhat inexperienced when they'd met, but not so innocent that she hadn't realized they were dynamite in bed together.

Their chemistry had been electric from the start.

She'd wanted to sleep with him on the first date. He'd kissed her at the doorstep, very sweetly, and she'd been tempted to invite him in. The second date, she had. Her roommate had come home early that night and almost caught them in a compromising position on the couch. Again, he'd left her wanting more.

On the third date, they'd barely made it through dinner.

She couldn't eat a bite. He'd just stared at her. She'd brought him home afterward, and they hadn't bothered with coffee or a nightcap. She'd taken him straight to her bedroom.

They'd been insatiable, and not just in the physical sense. He couldn't get enough of her, intellectually. Sean wasn't a big talker, but he was a great listener. He shared a little and she shared a lot. They'd connected on so many levels.

Over the years, the passion between them hadn't cooled, but it had transformed into something deeper and more intimate.

Their relationship also had its ups and downs, like any other. She wasn't crazy about the time he spent abroad. He didn't get along with her mother—at all. And Sean could be annoyingly taciturn when they argued. In response, she felt overemotional and shrill.

Her main complaint was that he didn't communicate with her. More often, he showed his feelings in a physical way. If he had a bad day, or a tough conversation with his father or even a week of poor surfing weather, he tended to internalize his frustration. Instead of talking about his struggles with her, he took what he needed from her in bed.

As faults went, it wasn't the worst one a man could have.

Sexual intimacy had been a strong component in their marriage. Too strong, perhaps. When she was no longer able to provide him that release, they'd faltered. She hadn't allowed him to touch her. He'd wanted to make everything better with sex. They'd never found a common ground.

They still hadn't. She wasn't foolish enough to think the emotional connection they'd made over the wounded seal pup had righted every wrong between them. Although his touch hadn't healed her broken heart, it *had* triggered the same earth-shattering sexual response she'd felt when they first kissed.

She wasn't over Sean, and she wasn't over their divorce. But she was definitely over the period of mourning that prevented her from feeling desire.

Her body was still humming from their encounter.

And he'd barely touched her. One kiss, a couple of quick strokes. God! She hadn't had sex in more than two years. She didn't want a whisper of a caress, or a few gentle strums from his fingertips.

She wanted his weight pressing her down. His hands gripping her hips. His hungry mouth all over her body.

She wanted every inch of him, filling her up, all night long.

Smothering a groan, she drained the tub and rose from the bath, her legs trembling. The stubbly towel on her pebbled skin felt like foreplay. She wrapped it around her wet hair and put on Sean's sweatpants and T-shirt, shivering.

There was a light rap of knuckles on the door. *His* knock. "Dani?"

She opened the door, arranging her features into a cool expression. What she really wanted to do was jump on him.

He kept his eyes trained on her face. "Jason's sleeping downstairs tonight. I thought you should stay in my room."

She wasn't going to argue with him there. "How did the railing look?" she asked, following him into the hallway.

"Suspicious. Jason called the Coast Guard."

In his room, she sat down on the bunk where they'd just gotten each other off. He shut the door and locked it. Her mind should have been on the ordeal they faced, and the near-drowning she'd just experienced. It wasn't.

She hugged her arms around herself. "What's it like here during a storm?"

"Depends."

"On what?"

"Duration, amount of precipitation, wind speed, wave height."

She sighed, accustomed to this type of answer from him. His view of the world relied heavily on surfer science. "Is it scary?"

"Yes, it's scary. And the charter boats stop bringing supplies. If the weather isn't too bad tomorrow, you can go back to San Francisco."

"I don't want to go back," she said.

His gaze cruised over her, lingering on her cheek. "I want you to be safe."

She touched her face, feeling self-conscious. There was a nasty scrape from the jagged rocks she'd been clinging to. It was noticeable, but nothing compared to the muscle strain and emotional trauma.

"I'm fine," she insisted, frustrated by his attempts to get rid of her. She couldn't leave without finding some kind of closure on their relationship. She knew he was scared, too—scared of taking another chance on her.

"I have every right to be worried."

Her spine stiffened. "No. You have no rights where I'm concerned. We're divorced. Remember?"

He made a harsh sound. "Yeah, I remember. How could I forget? The day you signed the papers I went out with Rob and got falling-down drunk. He picked up these two lonely girls, one for each of us. Instead of sleeping with her, I spent the night with my head in the toilet. I don't know what turned my stomach more—the alcohol I'd consumed, or the idea of having sex with a stranger in some pathetic attempt to forget you."

The world closed in around them, bringing this moment into sharp focus. Suddenly, she was short of breath. "What do you mean?"

"You're the one who wanted to split up. Not me."

"Then why did you file the papers?"

"Because I said I would. Because you didn't call. Because I thought—" He broke off, cursing. "I thought you wouldn't sign them. Stupid, right? I'd convinced myself that you would come running back to me, saying you couldn't live without me. That you'd made a mistake. That you—still loved me."

The remaining air rushed out of her chest. His words hurt so much, she almost couldn't bear it. She couldn't blame him for hating her. She hated *herself,* for what she'd put them through. "I'm sorry," she whispered, feeling like a broken record. "If it's any consolation, the decision wasn't easy for me, either. I thought I was doing what was best. I thought you wanted me to let you go."

He avoided her eyes. "You should get some rest."

While she was in the bath, he'd moved her stuff into his room. Her sleeping bag was on the lower bunk. She slipped inside it.

The air had grown cold.

He flipped the switch, casting the room into darkness. She wasn't surprised when he climbed into the top bunk. His reaction to the aftermath of their encounter, jerking away from her when she'd kissed his back, had spoken louder than words.

With Sean, actions always did.

Although she hadn't expected him to curl up next to her, or wrap his arms around her, she still ached from emptiness. She needed him so much. Not just his body. His comfort, his love, his acceptance, his strength.

And now she knew exactly how he'd felt, every time she'd pushed him away.

Chapter 14

The instant Sean awoke, he knew something was wrong. The room was pale with early morning light, and rain spattered the windowpane.

Daniela was in the lower bunk, fast asleep.

Then he heard Jason's muffled voice in the hall, along with the sound of hurried footsteps and opening doors. Frowning, Sean climbed down from the top bunk and pulled on his discarded trousers. Dani stirred, murmuring his name in her sleep. He crossed the room in two strides, opening the door to look out.

Jason was searching the other bedrooms, an anxious expression on his face. His hair stuck up on one side, and his pants were only half-buttoned. "Do you know where Elizabeth is?" he asked.

Sean could see into Elizabeth's room. Her bed looked rumpled, and empty. "No."

Jason moved on, ducking his head into Taryn's room. She blinked at him groggily. "Wh-what do you want?"

"I'm looking for Elizabeth."

She glanced around in confusion.

Jason made a sound of frustration and continued down the hall, to Brent's room. His door was closed, but unlocked. When Jason pushed it open, the edge of the door hit Brent's legs, which were hanging over the end of the bed.

Brent was so startled he got tangled up in his sleeping bag and fell off the other side. "What the hell?" he growled, lurching to his feet.

"Have you seen Elizabeth?"

"Not since last night."

"She's missing," Jason said.

Daniela came up beside Sean, her face showing concern. Taryn appeared in the doorway across the hall. Brent stood next to Jason, silent.

"Elizabeth is *missing*," he repeated. "Am I speaking English?"

"Well, she must be around here somewhere," Sean said, scratching his jaw. "Did you check outside?"

"Not yet."

"How did she get by you? I thought you were watching the front door."

Jason raked a hand through his hair, chagrined. "I fell asleep."

Sean walked down the hall, toward Elizabeth's room. He was no longer concerned with protecting her privacy. The safety of the crew took precedence.

Jason joined him, his expression grim. The room was small, and there wasn't much to snoop through. The closet, her laptop, a single suitcase. He opened the closet first. Two oars rested inside, propped against the wall.

Their eyes met.

"Holy Christ," Sean muttered, shocked to the core.

They searched the rest of the room quickly, finding nothing else of interest.

"Check her computer," Taryn suggested. "Maybe the daily logs can give us a clue about her state of mind."

Sean wasn't able to access her laptop without a password. On the top of Elizabeth's desk, however, there was a flash drive. He took it downstairs to the office computer, searching its contents.

Everyone gathered around the screen, curious.

Before he opened the logs, he noticed that a video file with Brent's name on it had recently been viewed. Sean pressed play. And encountered the most disturbing footage imaginable.

A burly redheaded man was swimming in turquoise waters. He wore no protective gear, just a tie-dyed tank top, old swim trunks and a snorkel. The mask was pushed up on his forehead. His shoulders were covered with brown freckles and patches of paler skin, as if he frequently burned and peeled.

Those details were peripheral to what was happening in the water. The guy was swimming with *sharks*. Not just any sharks, but some damned big ones. A group of ten-foot bulls darted around him aggressively, their tails stiff.

Sean recognized the sign of an impending attack. The man in the video ignored the warning signals. He didn't attempt to get out of the water, nor did he have the sense to stay still or be quiet. Laughing like a madman, he reached out to stroke the sharks' tails.

The viewer could tell that the footage was being filmed by a young man on the deck of a charter boat. Brent. His voice was that of an uncertain boy. He expressed concern over the man's reckless behavior, and several other tourists murmured their disapproval.

The actual attack was short and brutal.

One of the sharks struck, tearing at the man's legs. A bright burst of blood tainted the water. He hollered once and went white, going into shock almost immediately. Shrill cries rang out from the deck. Brent made a strange sound, like a whimper, but he held the camera steady.

Sean couldn't have said why the sharks didn't continue to attack. After what seemed like an agonizingly long interval, a safety ring was tossed to the man in the water. He was able to grab it. Two other men pulled him onto the deck.

His legs were severed from the knees down. The remaining flesh was hanging there like ragged clothes, in bloody, uneven tatters.

The boy Brent finally lost his composure. He turned away from the gruesome sight and ran to the side of the boat, where he became violently ill.

After the scene ended, Sean looked up, gauging the reactions of the rest of the crew. Daniela had her fist pressed to her mouth. Taryn was pale and silent. Jason flew across the room, going straight for Brent.

"She watched that," he said, slamming him into the living room wall. "How could you let her see that?"

Brent pushed him backward, holding his ground. "I didn't give it to her. She must have hacked into my files."

Jason grabbed him by the front of the shirt. "Why would you keep that on your laptop?"

Brent made a face. "I was trying to edit it a few weeks ago. Elizabeth's mother asked for a copy of the footage after he died. I thought I might be able to do some clever tricks to make it look less graphic."

Jason's hold loosened. There was no way to make that footage less graphic. But he couldn't fault Brent for trying. "I'm going to check the outbuildings," he said in a far-off voice. "If I don't find her in the next few minutes, we'll organize a search."

"Good idea," Sean said. "Taryn, why don't you get some coffee going? The rest of us will put our gear on."

She nodded smartly, and they all dispersed, ready to work as a team.

While Jason went out into the pounding rain, Sean followed Daniela back to his room, hoping that a search and rescue effort wouldn't be necessary. Shaken, he sat down in the chair and laced up his boots, trying not to watch her change clothes.

It was a lost cause. Out of the corner of his eye, he caught a glimpse of pale skin and black lace. She pulled on a pair of cargo pants and a thermal shirt before he could see more, but no amount of fabric could disguise her curves.

Her gaze met his, and he couldn't look away. Last night, he'd poured his heart out to her. Yesterday, she'd seen him cry. Today, he should have felt like a sentimental fool. He didn't. But the ease with which he was falling in love with her again—or perhaps just realizing he'd never fallen out of love—scared the hell out of him.

As soon as this was finished, and they were safe in San Francisco, he was going to have a serious talk with her. Not the fumbling, half-assed attempt at communication he usually managed, but a real conversation.

He wanted her back.

When she finished dressing, they went downstairs together, the sound of their footsteps echoing in the taut silence.

Jason came in from the rain a few moments later, shivering like a wet dog. He was breathing hard, from either panic or exertion, and his eyes were anxious.

Sean felt sorry for him. He'd been there, in that exact state of mind, and he wouldn't wish it on anyone.

Grabbing the polyurethane-sealed map from the back counter, Jason placed it on the table. "I didn't see any footprints, but it's raining pretty hard out there. Not much visibility from the tower, either. And there's no sign of her in the outbuildings."

"We should go to the bird blind first," Taryn recommended, taking a sip of coffee. "I bet she's there."

Jason nodded. "Why don't you and Brent head out that way? If she isn't at the blind, you can check the north side." He made a path on the map with his fingertip. "We found the skinned seal there."

Brent studied the general area and murmured his assent.

Jason tapped a point on the other side of the island. "As long as Daniela's up to it, you two can hit the sea lion blind and Dead Man's Beach."

Beside him, Daniela shivered. She was probably thinking about the lady in white, her pale limbs washed ashore. "Of course," she said. "I'm fine."

"I'll head up to the tower—"

"You should stay here," Sean said, cutting off Jason. "What if she comes back?"

Jason frowned. "I want to search."

"We don't want to miss a call from the Coast Guard," Brent added. "If you'd rather go with Taryn, I can stay."

Jason deliberated for a moment. "Okay. I know the terrain better than you, anyway. I want everyone to remain alert, and be aware of your surroundings. We have to consider the possibility that Elizabeth is emotionally unstable. Dangerous, even." He looked around the room, as if hoping someone would dispute the idea. No one did.

Sean left his coffee on the table. "Let's go."

Each team took a two-way radio, and Brent kept one on his belt. They left him alone in the house and stepped outside. The rain had begun to let up a little, but a group of dark clouds loomed on the horizon, promising more bad weather.

Sean led Daniela down the craggy cliffs, toward the sea lion blind.

They didn't see any evidence of Elizabeth there. The concrete structure offered protection from the wind and rain, so it seemed a likely choice for someone needing shelter, but there were dozens of other places to hide.

Every moment she stayed missing, the situation became more strained.

They moved on, checking for footprints on Dead Man's Beach. The surface was smooth and clean, a fresh, cool blanket of maize.

"Where do you think she went?" she said, dragging the tip of her boot through the stiff upper layer of sand.

He thrust his hands into his pockets, reluctant to answer.

Daniela thought about the conversation she'd had with Elizabeth at the lighthouse tower, remembering her distraught expression and her frightening proximity to the cliffs. "I feel sorry for her."

"Don't feel too sorry. I'd bet anything that she skinned the seal and rigged the railing. Not to mention sabotaging the engine."

"She's not over her father's death. Seeing that footage traumatized her."

He stared at the dark, stormy sea, pensive.

"I don't know what I'd do if you were attacked," she murmured.

An emotion she couldn't identify flickered in his brown eyes. "I would never take an unnecessary risk."

"Not on purpose."

He only shook his head, falling silent. She knew he

didn't like to talk about death. The idea that he could suffer a fatal accident, and prompt her next nervous breakdown, was too painful to consider.

She watched the waves roll in to the shore, heavy and ominous.

"Maybe I should get another aumakua necklace."

She jerked her gaze back to his, surprised. It was the first time he'd made a reference to Natalie's funeral.

The ceremony had taken place less than a month after the accident, and she'd been a zombie, too weak to walk. Sean had wanted to carry her, but she'd refused his support, relying on a hospital wheelchair instead.

She remembered watching him as he stood over the tiny coffin, paying his respects. At the nape of his neck, just above the collar of his dark suit, there was a simple leather cord. On it hung a fossilized shark tooth, known to many surfers as Hawaiian aumakua, or a protective spirit. He'd had the necklace since he was a boy and he never took it off.

Until that day.

Shoulders trembling with emotion, he'd torn the cord from his neck. After pressing his lips to the tooth, he'd knelt and placed it on the surface of the coffin.

Tears filled her eyes at the memory.

"I know you took her death harder than I did," Sean said. "You cried more, and you grieved longer. It made me feel like I didn't love her enough." He touched the hollow of his throat reflexively. "But I did."

Her heart clenched with sorrow, and she closed her eyes, feeling the hot spill of tears down her cheeks. The rain began to fall in earnest, pelting the hood of her jacket and perforating the surface of the sand.

He stepped forward, bringing her into the shelter of his arms, and she let him. She let him comfort her. Tucking her head against his chest, she clutched the front of his jacket and cried, absorbing his warmth and accepting his strength, hanging on to her man while the world came crashing down around them.

At long last, she allowed herself to be protected by him.

Then the radio at his waist crackled with distortion, interrupting the tender moment, and they broke apart.

Cursing, Sean took the receiver off his belt and brought it to his ear, trying to hear over the sound of the deluge.

"…check in."

It was Jason.

He spoke into the receiver. "This is Sean. Can you repeat, over?"

"I said I wanted everyone to check in."

Sean exchanged a glance with her. "No sign of Elizabeth here."

"Same on this side," Jason said. "We've got nothing. I think we should head in. Brent, can you notify the authorities?"

"Will do. Over."

After Sean signed off, they stared at each other for a long moment. She hadn't felt this close to him since the accident. It shamed her to admit that she had no idea what he'd gone through. She'd been so caught up in her own grief, she couldn't see his.

Everything that had happened over the past few days was worth it, for this single instance. This simple conversation.

"Thank you for telling me," she said, her hands on his face.

He smiled, pressing a kiss to her palm.

Their ability to discuss Natalie, even briefly, didn't make their child's death any less of a tragedy. Even so, Daniela felt as though a crushing weight had been lifted from her shoulders. Her daughter was a real person, loved and lost, rather than a sad, dark secret.

She wiped the tears from her cheeks, and they left the beach, hand in hand. All around them rain continued to fall, strong and steady, like the beating of a heart.

They all arrived at the house around the same time.

It was quiet inside, and the living room was deserted. Taryn ducked into the downstairs bathroom while Jason went upstairs, looking for Brent. Daniela frowned when she heard a sudden commotion.

Footsteps pounded down the hall, and Jason called out for help.

Sean ran up the stairs, taking two at a time. Pulse racing, Daniela followed him. At the end of the hallway, Brent was lying in a dark pool of his own blood. Jason crouched beside him, checking his pulse.

"Oh my God," Daniela said, her heart in her throat. "What do we do?"

"Get Taryn," Jason ordered. "She has EMT training."

Sean strode down the hall. "I'll grab the first aid kit."

Daniela could see blood pumping from the wound on his scalp, spreading across the hardwood floor. Swallowing back her nausea, she rushed into the bathroom, yanking several towels off the rack.

"And call 911!" Jason shouted at Sean.

Taryn ran down the hall, her face white with concern. Grabbing the towels from Daniela, she knelt beside Brent and held one to the laceration on the back of his scalp.

Daniela knew that head wounds bled a lot. But the injury looked severe, and he was unconscious. His breathing was shallow and uneven. His life was in danger.

Sean bounded back up the stairs, taking two at a time.

"Here," he said, setting down the red-and-white box that housed emergency supplies. "I don't think the phone is working. I couldn't get a dial tone."

Daniela's stomach flipped.

Jason looked up at Sean. "Let's try the shortwave."

After they hurried away to try the radio, Daniela focused her attention on Brent. Taryn lifted the towel from the back of his head. The wound was still seeping, but not so much that Daniela thought he would die from blood loss, rather than blunt force trauma.

With shaking hands, Taryn rummaged through the first aid kit. Tearing open a few packages of gauze, she placed the four-inch squares over the cut. If his skull was fractured, she might damage his brain, just by trying to stop the bleeding.

"I hope he'll be okay," Daniela said, her voice breaking.

The next few moments passed in a whirlwind of confusion. Daniela could hear Jason and Sean talking about cell phones, but no one had service. The laptops, with satellite internet, were also useless.

Both the house phone and the shortwave radio were dead.

There was a loud banging noise downstairs, as if someone had thrown a heavy object against the wall.

"How can I help?" Daniela asked.

Taryn took the pads of gauze away from Brent's head and inspected them. They were dotted with blood, but not soaked through. "We're going to have to move him," she murmured. "I think we should try to close the wound."

"With what?"

"Butterfly bandages," she decided. "There should be some in the kit."

Daniela searched the first aid supplies, finding several

small packages and handing them to Taryn. She tore them open with her teeth. The laceration started behind his left ear, running jagged along his hairline. "You have to hold it closed," Taryn said, removing the paper from the sticky adhesive strips. "But don't press too hard."

Daniela flinched at the command, but she didn't hesitate. With trembling fingers, she held the edges of the cut together, using a light touch, while Taryn applied the bandages. It was a patchwork job, but it would have to do until he got to the emergency room.

Taryn covered the bandage with fresh pads and secured them with white medical tape. "He needs a hat."

Daniela found several. They put a stretch knit beanie on him, followed by a sheepskin cap with convenient earflaps.

From the supply closet, Sean brought up a Stokes litter. It was the same kind of equipment used by the Coast Guard to transport and immobilize victims. Often suspended from a moving helicopter during an ocean rescue, the stretcher was sturdy, compact and buoyant. They rolled Brent onto it, using a brace to support his neck. With a clean, wet towel, Taryn wiped the blood from his handsome face. His eyes remained closed, his body unnaturally still. He never showed a flicker of consciousness.

A sob caught in Daniela's throat.

"We can't all go with him," Sean said, stating the obvious.

The whaler could hold five or six adults in clear weather, over a short distance. Under these conditions, three was the maximum, and the trip would be extremely dangerous.

"I'll drive," Jason said.

"I have CPR training," Taryn said. "I should go, too."

Sean didn't like it. He obviously wanted to go himself, but he couldn't leave Daniela on the island with a homicidal maniac. The choice was between sending two crew members out in a serious storm or letting Brent die here.

"He's in bad shape," Taryn urged. "We have to go now."

Jason took one end of the stretcher and Sean lifted the other, making their way down the stairs with care. Daniela covered his body with a waterproof safety blanket, protecting him from the elements. The journey from the house to the landing was bumpy and arduous, causing her to wince on Brent's behalf, but he didn't seem to mind. He showed no reaction to being jostled along the trail like a litter of supplies.

She swallowed past the lump in her throat, praying he would pull through. Finally, they had him loaded in the whaler, bundled up tight.

The sky was dark and heavy; the rain hadn't abated.

"Be careful," Sean said, shouting to be heard above the roar of the wind.

Taryn threw her arms around his neck, hugging him tight. "You too," she said, pressing her lips to his shadowed cheek. The emergency had stripped away some of her hard feelings, and Daniela was no longer stung by jealousy.

None of that mattered now. Sean didn't want a romantic relationship with Taryn, but he still cared about her. They were friends.

After giving Daniela the same kind of hug, warm and hopeful and more than a little frantic, Taryn climbed into the hull. Jason got behind the wheel and signaled to Sean with a nod, indicating that they were ready.

Sean operated the crane, lowering the whaler onto the raging sea. The boat bucked and swayed on the choppy surface. Taryn held on to the stretcher, trying to keep her body low. It was dangerous to launch in weather like this, and insane to navigate the notoriously tumultuous San Francisco Bay.

It was going to be a rough ride.

Jason managed to unhitch the hook, and they sped away. Taryn looked back, waving to Sean and Daniela as the boat got smaller and smaller. Eventually, they disappeared into the fog, like a ghostly apparition.

Chapter 15

The landing was no place to linger in the pouring rain. Sean put his hand on Daniela's arm, encouraging her to hurry, but she was frozen to the spot. The bizarre events of the past hour were catching up with her, the frightening implications sinking in.

They were stranded.

Jason and Taryn could reach San Francisco Bay this afternoon, if they were lucky, but no rescue team would be dispatched until the weather improved. A visit from the Coast Guard was unlikely. Air support, impossible.

They were stuck here, on Southeast Farallon, with no transportation and no means of communication.

Knowing a crazy person was on the loose made her panic increase tenfold, and being surrounded by shark-infested waters didn't help. The island seemed to shrink, closing in on her. She couldn't breathe. Her heart pounded with anxiety and her lungs refused to expand.

There was no hope. No help. No escape.

"Look at me," Sean ordered, taking her by the upper arms and shaking her gently. "Damn it, Dani, stay with me."

She blinked a few times, watching his face waver in and out of focus.

"Brent is going to be fine. You're going to be fine. We're all going to be fine. But I need your help. I need you to stay strong."

Her legs felt like rubber, incapable of supporting her, but she closed her eyes and visualized a safer, happier place. Laguna Nigel, on their honeymoon. Beautiful, sunny beaches. Soft summer breezes and warm sand beneath her feet.

Managing to suck in a quick breath, she opened her eyes. "Okay."

His relief was palpable. "I can carry you, but I'd rather have my hands free."

She didn't need him to explain why. "I can walk," she said, shaking her head. This was no time for fainting and hyperventilating. After another moment of concentration, she was able to set her fear aside.

Taking a steadying breath, she started down the path, heading toward the house. The rain hammered against her hood and the wind tugged at her jacket like a menacing hand, inviting her to lose her balance on the uneven ground, to skirt closer to land's edge.

Rivers of water appeared everywhere, coursing across the footpaths. In some areas, it was like wading through a creek bed.

She trudged forward, putting one foot in front of the other, trying to stay alert. With Sean behind her, protecting her back, it was up to her to watch out for a frontal attack. Breathe, she told herself. Just breathe.

At the bottom of the trail, she almost slipped and fell. Sean reached out to grab her upper arm, holding her upright. "Steady now?"

She moistened her lips. "Yes."

The inside of the house brought instant relief from the elements. After making sure the downstairs was clear of intruders, Sean locked the front door. Rifling through the supply closet, he located the tagging equipment he and Jason had used a few days ago.

It seemed like weeks.

"Take this," Sean said, handing her one of the sleek metal poles. It was sturdy, but not too unwieldy to swing.

He kept the other for himself.

"I'm going to check upstairs."

"I'm coming with you," she said immediately.

"No. This is the easiest area to defend. In the bedrooms, there are too many places to hide."

"I'll stand at the top of the stairs."

His jaw clenched with displeasure, but he nodded, making a compromise. They went up the stairs together, moving in unison. At the edge of the hallway, he inched away from her. Her heart went with him.

Be careful! her mind screamed. She had the frantic urge to tell him she loved him. Gripping the smooth metal bar in her hands, she bit down on her lower lip, forcing herself to remain silent.

He stepped into the bathroom, his legs braced wide. It was unoccupied.

The room she shared with Taryn was also empty. He pushed the door against the wall to make sure. Sean and Jason's room was trickier, as it had a closet. He had to go all the way inside, disappearing completely from her view.

Seconds ticked by in taut silence. Blood roared in her ears and her palms grew slick with sweat. Her eyes darted from the stairway to the hall and back again. Finally, he reappeared, shaking his head.

She let out the breath she'd been holding.

Brent's room was neat as a pin, his duffel bag sitting on top of the crisply made bed. In contrast, Elizabeth's room appeared to have been ransacked. From where she stood, Daniela could see clothes on the floor.

"All clear," Sean said.

Daniela relaxed her stance, loosening her grip on the pole.

"Maybe Elizabeth came back to confront him while we were out."

After giving the floor a brief inspection, she crossed the room, glancing out the rain-splattered window. It wasn't yet noon, but the sky was so dark, it might as well have been dusk. "Do you really think she did it?"

"I don't know who else could have. I don't see a weapon here, either."

Elizabeth must have taken it with her. A chilling thought. "I guess she wanted to avenge her father."

"Yeah, but she put all of us in danger. Not just Brent."

They closed the bedroom doors and went back downstairs. While Sean made a pot of tea, she sat down on the couch, her legs tucked beneath her and the tagging spear close by. It was difficult for her to remain calm. With no important tasks to distract her, she couldn't help but replay the terrifying morning, and imagine a dozen future horrors.

Sean handed her a steaming mug. "Here."

Although she longed for something stronger, like his warm hands all over her body, she accepted the tea and took an experimental sip.

"Are you okay?"

No. "Yes."

"I'm going to take another look at the radio. Maybe I can fix it."

She nodded mutely. In this weather, the Coast Guard wouldn't come unless they were out in the middle of the ocean. Like Taryn and Brent and Jason. Having a line of communication with the authorities could save their lives, though.

Daniela shuddered, considering the terrible danger the others faced.

Sean brought a multicolored blanket out from the supply closet, wrapping it around her like a hug. The thick wool smelled like sun and sand, as if someone had taken it to the beach on a warm summer afternoon.

"Try not to worry," he murmured, kissing the top of her head.

She stared up at him, too tense to smile. They had a long day ahead, followed by another endless night.

Sean didn't have any luck with the radio. There were parts missing and wires all over the place. He thought about crossing some of the loose wires, trying to create a basic SOS signal, but he didn't know which ones to choose.

He was a scientist, not an electrician.

The phone lines were a different story. If they'd been cut, he could splice the edges together and slap on some electrical tape. If the satellite receiver had been damaged, they were probably SOL.

His other option was to destroy the signal at the lighthouse tower. Elizabeth wasn't the only one who could trash equipment. Sean could make short work of the automated beacon, rendering it useless in minutes.

Interfering with the signal would create a major stir at Coast Guard Headquarters, and it probably wouldn't cause any shipwrecks. Most boats were equipped with GPS, making lighthouse technology obsolete.

Smaller vessels needed the beacon, however, especially in an emergency situation, and he didn't want to put any more lives in danger.

He'd done enough of that.

If Taryn and Jason didn't make it to San Francisco, he'd never forgive himself. There were a lot of rough patches between here and there, and Brent was seriously injured. Worrying about them made Sean's blood pressure skyrocket, so he tried to stay positive.

Having a stress-induced heart attack wouldn't keep Daniela safe.

To his surprise, she'd fallen asleep. For the past two hours, while he'd been fidgeting with the radio and thumbing through repair manuals, she'd been breathing softly, snuggled deep in the wool blanket.

She looked so damned adorable. He wanted to kiss her lush little mouth and slide his hands beneath her cozy blanket.

Because she needed the rest, he didn't touch her.

After several moments of watching her sleep, and thinking of all the dirty things he'd like to do to her, he put on his jacket, moving quietly toward the door. If he woke her, she'd insist on going outside with him. And he'd only be gone a minute.

He disengaged the lock and rotated the doorknob, very gently…

"What are you doing?"

Damn. Turning to face her, he said, "I was just going to check the phone lines. See if they've been cut."

She straightened, running a hand through her mussed hair. Her eyes were half-lidded from sleep, her mouth curved into a sexy pout. Even when she was mad, she was beautiful. "What if I'd woken up while you were gone?"

He thought fast. "I'd have been back before you had a chance to worry."

With a groan, she stood, letting the blankets fall away from her. "You're not going anywhere without me."

He held up a hand, warding her off. "Dani, this will take sixty seconds, tops. It doesn't make any sense for us both to go. You're safer here, and I don't want to have to search the rooms again."

After a moment of hesitation, she nodded. "I'll stand right here at the door."

"Fine." He waited while she donned her jacket and grabbed the tagging spear, wielding it like a baton. His was resting beside the door. Instead of picking it up, he reached for her, needing one more thing before he left.

He took her in his arms and kissed her, hard. She made a little sound of surprise and melted against him, parting her soft lips. Taking advantage of the opportunity, he swept his tongue inside, plundering her sweet mouth again and again.

The metal pole slipped from her hands, clanging to the floor.

By the time he lifted his head, she was out of breath, speechless. He rubbed his thumb over her kiss-swollen lips, but he didn't say anything. In this situation, "I love you" sounded fatalistic.

"Be careful," she said.

"I will."

He was good on his word, avoiding blind corners and staying alert. In the pouring rain, it was easy to get snuck up on, so he watched his back, too. Knowing that Dani was waiting for him kept him moving fast. He didn't want to let her down.

As far as he could tell, the phone lines were intact. If the satellite receiver was broken, there was no easy solution for that.

Cursing, he beat a hasty retreat back to the house.

She shut the door and locked it behind him, shivering from cold. "Can you fix it?"

He took off his wet jacket. "I doubt it. I think it's the satellite. At first light, I'll go up to the tower and have a look."

"What about the radio?"

"Parts are missing. And I'm no MacGyver."

"Is there anything else we can do tonight?"

"I could wreck the lighthouse beacon," he admitted, "but the Coast Guard probably wouldn't investigate the incident until the weather improved."

She nibbled on her lower lip, worried. "So we'll just have to wait it out?"

Eyes on her mouth, he nodded, thinking of a dozen ways to distract her, all of which were wildly inappropriate for a life-or-death situation. "Cell phone reception is better at the tower, too. When the rain lets up, we can give that a go."

"Okay," she said, relaxing her shoulders. "When the rain lets up."

It was going to be a long night.

"Are you hungry?" he asked, trying to reroute his appetite to food, rather than sex. They'd skipped breakfast, and missed lunch. "I think it's my turn to cook."

"We should eat something," she agreed.

He made grilled cheese sandwiches while she heated up a can of vegetable soup. The meal they prepared wasn't fancy, but it was hot, and he was hungrier than he thought. He ate his sandwich and half of hers.

The rain continued to come down hard, hammering

the roof and gushing from the rain gutters, making the confines of the house seem cozier, more intimate. As she washed the dishes, his eyes were drawn to the nape of her neck, silky-pale in contrast to her dark hair, and the enticing curve of her bottom.

He couldn't prevent himself from fantasizing about tugging down the back of her pants and pressing his lips to that cute little scar. Tracing it with his tongue.

She turned away from the sink, drying her hands on a towel.

It took him a half a second to drag his gaze up to her face. Her cheeks were flushed. She moistened her lips.

"I think I'll wash up," he rasped.

A tiny crease formed between her brows. "Are you going to shave?"

He rubbed a hand over his jaw, encountering about a week's worth of stubble. Out here, he preferred some protection from the elements. "Do you want me to?"

"No."

His gaze fell again, lingering on the swells of her breasts, the apex of her thighs. He used to shave every day, just to please her. On certain occasions, however, he'd come home scruffy as hell, and she'd welcomed him that way, too.

Enthusiastically, as he recalled.

"Fine," he said, clearing his throat. "Come with me, though. I'll feel better if we stick close together."

She nodded, following him upstairs. He left the bathroom door open while he leaned over the sink, washing his face. Considering his next step.

He wanted Daniela, but he was afraid of screwing things up again. The events that preceded their divorce had been incredibly painful for both of them. One disturbing memory, in particular, kept resurfacing.

The year after the accident, Dani hadn't interacted with

him, or anyone else, on an intimate level. When he tried to talk with her, she avoided his company. She wouldn't let him touch her. She rarely even made eye contact.

It was like living with a ghost.

He suspected that she wished she'd died with Natalie, and although he'd never voiced this fear, he'd been terrified that she would commit suicide.

Months passed this way, until he couldn't stand the distance between them. He started pressing her harder, insisting she spend more time with him. He'd badger her into taking a walk on the beach. Instead of going surfing alone, he'd beg her to swim with him in the ocean. He'd do anything to get her out in the sunshine.

One day, they had a breakthrough. He hadn't planned anything special, just a stroll in the park and a quiet dinner at a romantic restaurant. They saw a lot of babies that afternoon. It was difficult for her, but impossible to avoid. When they got home, he poured her a glass of wine and sat down next to her on the couch, expecting a typical evening.

She'd seemed distracted, not really paying attention to the book she was reading, so he leaned over and kissed her on the lips. To his surprise, she didn't shy away.

For the first time in over a year, she kissed him back.

He wasn't sure how it happened, but one moment they were sharing a simple kiss, the next he had his hands all over her. Not touching her for so long had a predictable effect on his self-control. Maybe if he'd been a little less eager, he could have prevented one of the biggest mistakes of his life. But he loved her so much it *hurt,* and having her in his arms again felt so right. He was desperate to keep her there. In that moment, he'd have promised her anything. Whatever she wanted. Another baby.

He hadn't realized he'd made the suggestion out loud

until she froze, retracting in horror. Right before his eyes, she retreated into herself, becoming distant and inaccessible, her heart locked away inside. All the work he'd done over the past few weeks was erased in one fell swoop. Destroyed with one misspoken sentiment.

The next day, she'd asked for a separation.

He'd panicked, trying to explain his position. He didn't care about having a baby, but he cared about sex, and he cared about *her*. "I can't go on like this," he'd said, growing desperate. "I love you too much not to touch you."

She'd covered her face with one hand, shaking her head.

"Don't you love me anymore?" he asked, his voice a tortured whisper. He'd never felt so vulnerable in his entire life.

"I think you should move out," was all she said. Breaking his heart. Destroying his ego. And bringing back the most painful memory of his childhood.

While he was growing up, his parents had fought nonstop. His father had always yelled and cursed and complained, and his mom hadn't exactly been a delicate flower. She'd given it back as good as she got it.

He remembered, very clearly, the day his mother had asked his father to leave the house. His old man hadn't gone quietly, either. He'd railed against her, calling her a coldhearted bitch in one breath and falling to his knees the next, begging for her to reconsider.

She hadn't.

Sean refused to exhibit that kind of behavior. He would never be the kind of man who raised his voice to a woman; he'd rather walk away. Groveling wasn't his style, either. Instead of arguing with Daniela about the separation, or pleading his case, he'd merely promised to see a lawyer and packed his things.

Looking back, he realized that his inability to articulate his true feelings, for fear of appearing weak and pathetic, like his father, had been the nail in the coffin of their relationship. He might not have been able to hold their marriage together without her cooperation, but he could have tried harder. Communicated better. Waited longer.

Sean pushed away from the sink now, running a thin towel over his face. He put on a clean T-shirt and opened the medicine cabinet, rifling through its contents. There was a box of condoms inside, probably left there by Jason. Appreciating his foresight, Sean checked the expiration date to make sure they were still good and pocketed a few.

Closing the cabinet door, he studied his reflection in the mirror, taking a good, hard look at himself. He'd promised to love, honor and protect Dani, for richer or poorer, in sickness and in health, as long as they lived.

He wanted to follow through on that vow.

After a brief hesitation, he turned his back to the mirror and walked away from the past, making his decision.

Daniela sat at the top of the stairwell, her elbows planted on her knees, waiting for Sean to come out of the bathroom.

When he did, his eyes met hers, and her heart skipped a beat.

His clothes were worn and faded, his jaw scruffy. He looked fantastic clean-shaven, but there was something so appealing about his rugged style and earthy masculinity when he was working in the field.

Even dirty, he was sexy.

He continued down the hall, grabbing both of their sleeping bags out of his room.

Last night he'd smelled delicious, like cold ocean water

and hot male skin. As he passed by her, she inhaled through her nostrils, straining for that scent.

"We should sleep downstairs," he said. "And block the front door."

She felt a flutter of nerves as she followed him, and not just because she'd rather be in a private bedroom with him than on a couch by the front windows.

They were going to have to talk.

Saying nothing, he moved the bookcase across the room, barricading the only door. The dual-pane windows would be very difficult for an intruder to get through. After a glance outside, he pulled the curtains shut and turned off all the lights except the one in the hall. He probably didn't want to advertise their presence. She sat down on the couch, hugging her knees to her chest, and he settled in next to her.

Putting his arm around her, he stroked her back while they listened to the rain.

The last time they were alone together like this, she'd been eight months pregnant. She remembered him splaying his hands over her belly and touching his lips to her neck, waiting for the baby to kick.

"Where do you think Elizabeth is?" she asked, resting her head on his shoulder.

"I don't know. I wish I did."

"She must be cold."

Out in the open, she was a likely candidate for hypothermia, and that condition wouldn't help her think more clearly. If they didn't get help soon, she could die. Daniela regretted not being able to continue the search.

She murmured a quick prayer, making a sign of the cross.

Sean had never been religious. She too had found little comfort in faith after their daughter's death, so she couldn't fault him for it. Now, instead of offering her empty assurances, he gave her his open arms, enveloping her in quiet strength.

She clung to the front of his shirt, blinking the tears from her eyes. Every time she looked at him, she was reminded of the way he'd touched her last night. Her body ached in secret places, hungry for more, and her heart swelled inside her chest, burdened with an impossible longing.

She loved him so much.

And she knew it was too late. She couldn't ask him for a second try, or another chance. But maybe he would grant her some…closure.

Taking a deep breath, she snuggled closer to him, twining her arms around his neck. Beneath her fingertips, his muscles were tense. She could see the pulse point at the base of his throat, beating strong and fast.

They both wanted this.

In that moment, she didn't want to analyze her emotions. She didn't want to talk about broken dreams and lost souls. She didn't want to consider the possibility that they would leave this place, and never see each other again.

She didn't want to think—she wanted to *feel*.

But she knew she owed him her compete honesty, and her best effort. This was no time to be subtle or halfhearted. The stakes were too high.

"I love you," she said, her lips against his ear. "I love you, and I want you."

His entire body went rigid. "You…what?"

"I want you." She touched her tongue to his throat, tasting salt. "Desperately. I hate the way things ended between us." His pulse throbbed beneath her parted lips. "I'm not asking you to take me back for good, but I would do anything to make it up to you. I'd give anything for one more night."

"Just…one night?"

"Yes," she said, panting against the wet spot her mouth had made.

He thrust his hands in her hair, forcing her to meet his eyes. "No."

"No?"

"I could never be satisfied by one night," he said, and kissed her.

Chapter 16

"I love you, too," Sean said, dragging his mouth from hers. "I never stopped loving you. I will *always* love you."

Daniela should have been all cried out, but fresh tears filled her eyes. "You will?"

He kissed her again. "Yes. But one night isn't enough. I want to have you, over and over again. I want you, every part of you, forever."

His words sent a thrill of pleasure down her spine. At the same time, she was afraid to pin her hopes on a shared future with him. She didn't believe in happily ever after anymore. And there was no such thing as forever.

She hesitated. "Sean—"

"Never mind," he growled, taking her mouth again. "Don't say anything. Tonight, I don't want to hear you say anything but yes."

She climbed over his lap, accepting those terms, and he tightened his fingers in her hair, silencing her with a crushing kiss. With a low moan, she plastered her breasts against his chest and curled her tongue around his, returning his passion, sharing his desire.

Daniela wanted him to tear her clothes off, but when the kiss ended, he let his hands fall away from her. To her intense disappointment. "Tell me if I move too fast," he said, sounding uncertain. "I don't want to…push too hard."

His consideration for her feelings touched her deeply. And she also felt a pang of regret, for being the cause of his self-doubt.

"I want you to push me," she said, shifting her weight on his lap. "Hard."

His eyes darkened.

"Hard," she repeated, brushing her lips over his.

Groaning, he thrust his hands into her hair and his tongue inside her mouth, kissing her good and hard, like a man who'd been starving for the taste of a woman. Like a man who thought he'd never get enough.

She shivered with anticipation.

He'd never had any trouble fulfilling her needs sexually. In the bedroom, he'd always given her exactly what she wanted. And what she wanted now was to surrender to sensation. To strip her mind of paralyzing fears and painful memories.

"Make me forget," she said, pulling her shirt over her head. His gaze dropped from her mouth to her breasts. Farallon Island was no place for skimpy lingerie, but her intimate apparel was a little less utilitarian than her outerwear. Although supportive, her bra was made of stretchy black satin, edged in lace.

And, to be honest, she could wear a gunny sack and he'd love it.

Growling his approval, he splayed his hands over her

rib cage, just underneath her breasts. They swelled at his touch, threatening to spill over the cups of her bra, and her nipples pebbled against the silky fabric.

Moaning, she fisted her hands in his hair and arched her back, pressing her breasts against his face. Needing no further encouragement, he nuzzled her hungrily, trailing kisses along the lacy border of her bra.

She reached behind her back, unfastening the clasp. When her breasts tumbled free, he groaned, filling his hands with her soft flesh. He also filled his mouth, flicking his tongue over one dusky tip, then the other.

"Yes," she said, squirming on his lap. "God, yes."

His erection swelled against the apex of her thighs, and she moved back and forth, rubbing herself along the hard length. Seeking heat. Wanting more.

Frustrated by the layers of clothing between them, she tugged at his shirt. He released her breasts, raising his arms over his head to assist her. She tossed the shirt aside and flattened her palms over his chest, making a soft sound of appreciation. His skin was hot and smooth, his muscles bunched beneath her fingertips.

She bit down on his lower lip, tugging gently. "Take off your pants."

The corner of his mouth tipped up at her command. He stood, letting her body slide along the length of his in a slow, delicious drag. She watched, moistening her lips, while he unfastened the buttons on his weatherproof trousers and pushed them down to his knees. His erection tented the front of his boxer briefs.

Heat pooled to her lower body, making her legs feel wobbly. Smothering another moan, she wrestled with her own pants, kicking them out of the way. Her panties were black satin with lace trim, like her bra. He stared at the apex of her thighs, his Adam's apple bobbing in agitation, and she felt the fabric there get wet.

Hooking her thumbs in the waistband, she stripped them off.

Equally impatient, he shoved his briefs down and reached into the pocket of his trousers, finding a single condom. After stretching it over his jutting erection, he was good to go. With his pants around his ankles and his boots still on, he should have looked ridiculous.

He didn't.

No heterosexual woman on earth could gaze upon his naked body and think anything but *Oh my God* or *Come to Mama.*

Panting with excitement, she lay down on the couch, a soft pile of pillows and blankets behind her back. He sank his knee into the cushion between her parted thighs, positioning himself over her.

"If we do this too fast, I might not get the chance to make you forget," he said, his voice strained.

She curved her arms around his neck. "Then go slow."

He began to enter her, gritting his teeth. "Slow…and hard?"

"Just fill me up," she moaned, wrapping her legs around him. She wanted his mouth covering hers, his hands on her body, his skin against her skin. "Don't give me too much space. The last thing I need is more space."

He buried himself in her with a low groan, letting her feel every inch. "That's…perfect. I don't think there's any room to spare."

That was true, and always had been. They fit together exceedingly well.

In fact, after such a long stint of abstinence, he seemed larger. If she hadn't been so ready, she might have had trouble accommodating him. As it was, her slick, hot sex grasped him snugly, delighting in the invasion.

Judging by the look on his face, he was sharing her ecstasy. He paused, closing his eyes and savoring the sensation. "It's been so long, I'd forgotten how good this feels."

Her tummy quivered. "Really? How long has it been?"

"You know."

"There hasn't been anyone else?"

A muscle in his jaw ticked. He shook his head.

"For me either," she said, tightening her legs around his waist. "It's always been you. Just you. Only you."

He lowered his mouth to hers, kissing her passionately. Possessing her completely. Then he began to move. Keeping his word, he gave it to her slow *and* hard, drawing himself out of her with deliberate lassitude, driving back in with enough force to test the couch's frame. Every time his pelvis bumped into hers, she experienced a jolt of bone-melting pleasure. His control was impressive, his body was amazing and the friction was exquisite.

Outside, the rain pounded against the windows and the wind shrieked around the house, hammering the rooftop.

Inside, they were generating so much heat he was sweating. She raked her nails down his rock-hard pecs and over his clenched stomach muscles, admiring his form. With a strangled growl, he switched positions, sitting back on the couch and bringing her over his lap. He was obviously trying to last longer, and she could take him even deeper this way.

When she reseated herself, they both groaned at the sensation.

All restraint gone, she threw her head back and tilted her hips forward, saying yes. Panting for release. He gave it to her. Licking the pad of his thumb, he pressed it to her clitoris, moving in slow circles.

Her sex pulsed around his, gripping him tightly.

She dug her fingernails into his shoulders and screamed his name, shattering into a thousand pieces. Unable to hold on a moment longer, he came with her, a hoarse cry wrenching from his throat as he shuddered against her.

For a long time afterward, she held him close, hugging his head to her chest and stroking the nape of his neck.

Savoring this respite, while the storm raged on outside.

Chapter 17

At dawn, he woke her.

"Seems like the rain's letting up," Sean said, shaking her gently. "This may be the only chance we get."

Daniela blinked, trying to clear her vision. She felt as though she'd just closed her eyes. They'd made love several times, and slept only a few hours between them, but he didn't appear haggard in the least.

He looked ready to pounce.

With a tool belt around his waist, work boots on his feet, and his body poised for action, he exuded strength and determination.

He'd always been raring to go in the morning.

Groaning, she disentangled herself from the blankets, searching the immediate area for her clothes. She'd been sleeping in his flannel shirt and a pair of knee-high socks.

"That's a good look for you," he murmured, ogling her bare thighs.

She yawned, treating him with a view of her naked bottom as she rifled through her overnight bag. When she found a pair of cotton bikini briefs, she tugged them on, along with yesterday's pants and her waterproof boots. Fighting off the remnants of sleep, she stood, stretching her muscles.

His expression grew troubled. "Are you sore?"

"Not really."

"I'm sorry if I was too rough last night."

"Sean," she chided. "Stop."

"It's no wonder you didn't want me pawing you after the accident, exhausting you with my insatiable appetite—"

Laughter bubbled up from within her, spilling over. It was inappropriate, but irrepressible. "In case you didn't notice, I was just as insatiable as you were. I love your appetite. That was never the problem."

"Then…what was?"

She sobered, raking a hand through her hair. They'd had six months of grief counseling, during which she'd tried to sort through her feelings and he'd suffered in silence. Their sexual relationship had never been a topic of discussion. Sean wouldn't open up to the therapist at all, and Daniela's biggest concern had been keeping her head above water.

She'd assumed that her desire for him would come back eventually. And it had. Little by little, it had.

"Do you remember that night you kissed me, before the separation?"

"Of course. I pushed too hard—"

"No. I wanted you, too. But the instant you said 'baby,' I shut down."

He shook his head, cursing himself.

"A slip of the tongue, you claimed, but it sounded like a

voiced wish. And I couldn't take it anymore. Every time I looked at you, I was reminded of Natalie. Every time you got close to me, I felt claustrophobic." Although she knew she was hurting him, she had to say the words out loud. So they could move on. "At that point, I couldn't see past my own grief. I thought I was going to be miserable forever. I told myself that you were better off without me." She forced herself to meet his gaze. "I knew you deserved a woman who would make you happy. Accept your touch. Give you a family."

He took her by the hand. "I told you I don't care about that. You're my family. You're the only one I need."

She closed her eyes, feeling tears spill onto her cheeks. When she opened them, she watched for his reaction carefully. "You don't care about having children?"

It was a difficult question, and he struggled with his response. "I don't know, Dani. I don't have any expectations right now, to be honest. I *do* know that I can't live without you. And I know I can live without everything else."

"Okay," she said, letting out a breath.

"Okay, what?"

"Once we get back to San Francisco, I want to work this out." She smiled, hugging him. "No more space between us."

He held her close for a long moment. "I love you."

"I love you, too."

Daniela felt good about the decision. This wasn't a lukewarm reconciliation, or a halfhearted effort. They were full steam ahead, sexually. And they'd always been crazy in love. If they needed a bit of help with communication, that was okay.

She still wasn't sure what the future held, or even what the afternoon would bring, but she felt more hopeful than ever.

If they could make it off this island, they could overcome any obstacle.

"I'm going to check the damage on the satellite receiver," he said, helping her into her jacket. "Maybe it will be a simple repair. While I'm doing that, I want you to watch my back. Brent got snuck up on yesterday."

She nodded, moistening her lips. The tagging spears they'd been carrying around last night doubled as walking sticks, so they brought them along. He pushed aside the bookcase and unlocked the door, stepping outside warily. She followed at his signal, a cold wind blowing the hair off her forehead.

The rain had turned the world gray. It was falling lightly now, the dark sky swollen with still more. Rivulets of water trickled across the rocky ground beneath her feet, taking what little soil the island had with it.

Sean looked out past the landing, where powerful waves crashed along the jagged shoreline, sending sprays of saltwater high into the air.

"Do you think they made it?" she asked, shivering.

"I hope so," he said, his jaw clenched.

It went without saying that he'd never forgive himself if they hadn't. The other crew members were so young. They had their entire lives ahead of them.

The only alternative would have been to let them stay here on the island while she and Sean took Brent to the mainland. Either way, there was danger. Daniela could only pray they'd made the right choice.

In grim silence, they ascended the path, heading toward the lighthouse tower, moving carefully over the sliding earth. Rain continued to fall, soft but relentless. Her face became damp and her mind cleared.

She continued walking, sucking in deep breaths of frigid air.

As they rounded the last corner, he took her elbow, helping her past the precarious drop near the Washtub. When he released her, she climbed the remaining steps slowly, filled with a strong sense of foreboding.

Before inspecting the satellite equipment, he crept into the lighthouse tower, gesturing for her to stay back. The structure offered some protection from the wind and rain, and they couldn't play it too safe.

Elizabeth might be hiding somewhere, crouched to strike.

To Daniela's relief, the tower was uninhabited. Sean reappeared beside her, taking his cell phone out of his front pocket.

"Anything?"

He shook his head, pressing buttons. "No service."

"Damn."

With a sigh, he put the phone away and propped his tagging spear against the wall. He needed his hands free to check the satellite receiver, which was just outside the tower, about twenty feet away.

"I'll be right back," he promised, kissing her cheek. Her insides warmed at the feel of his facial hair, a firm bristle against her delicate skin. She knew she bore the faint marks of his whiskers in other, more intimate, places on her body.

Clearing her throat, she nodded. "I'll stay right here."

With due diligence, she watched him traverse the short distance from the tower to the satellite disk. Like the radio, it appeared to have been smashed. They couldn't communicate with the authorities.

She hoped Sean could fix it.

Instead of staring at his back, Daniela turned her eyes toward the path and kept her weapon at the ready, guarding her man like an armed sentry. With a panoramic view of the island, there was a lot of ground to cover, but very little chance she could miss a sneak attack. Behind the tower, there were only sheer cliffs, impossible to climb. Before her, there was a single footpath.

And yet, the sinking sensation refused to leave her. She wouldn't feel safe until they were back inside the house. Maybe even back under the covers.

Taking slow, even breaths, she continued to scan the hillside, frequently checking back on Sean. After a few tense moments, she caught a flash of movement.

Elizabeth.

She must have been standing on the narrow ledge behind the tower, her back flattened against the opposite wall, a frightening precipice at her feet. Sean hadn't even checked there; the daring hiding place hadn't occurred to either of them.

While Daniela watched, frozen with horror, Elizabeth rushed toward Sean, holding a wicked-looking hatchet over her head. Until now, Daniela hadn't been sure that the cool redhead was responsible for harming Brent. She'd considered the cage-diving crew unlikely suspects, but Elizabeth hadn't seemed violent.

One glimpse of her, wild-haired and wild-eyed, changed Daniela's mind.

"Watch out!" she screamed, her heart in her throat.

Sean turned, his eyes widening in surprise. He reacted quickly, scrambling backward to avoid a blow.

"Leave the equipment alone," Elizabeth said, baring her teeth.

Sean stopped retreating, his stance defensive. He had some sharp tools in his belt, but he didn't reach for them.

Daniela was several strides away from the pair. She stumbled forward, tightening her grip on the tagging spear.

Elizabeth turned her head toward the sound. "Don't come any closer," she said, the blade of the hatchet gleaming.

"We aren't going to hurt you," Sean said.

Daniela hesitated, praying that Elizabeth would be reasonable. "Put down the hatchet and talk to us. Maybe we can help."

Elizabeth laughed, shaking her head. "The only help I need is in shutting down this hellhole for good."

Sean and Daniela exchanged a worried glance. Apparently, Elizabeth was experiencing a mental breakdown. She'd succumbed to the pressures of this stressful, treacherous place. "Let's talk inside the house, where you can warm up," he said, inching toward her. "Put down the weapon. Please."

Elizabeth wavered, gripping the hatchet in her gloved hands. Her clothes were wet and her face was dirty. She looked lost and cold and confused.

"We can help you," he murmured, stepping closer.

But the instant his hand touched her shoulder, she exploded into action, swinging the hatchet over her head. He reacted just as quickly, blocking the attack. The descending blade made contact with his forearm, sinking into his flesh. The sleeve of his jacket split open. In an instant, his forearm was soaked in blood.

Daniela cried out, running toward them.

As Sean moved backward, trying to avoid further injury, Daniela charged, hitting Elizabeth with all the strength she possessed. The tactic worked. The tagging spear struck her like a javelin, impaling the middle of her stomach.

Screaming in pain, Elizabeth tumbled over the side of the cliff.

Momentum propelled Daniela, who was still holding the spear, right off the edge with her. She released the weapon a second too late, flailing wildly as she plummeted through the air, praying she'd clear the shore. Thankfully, the cliff face was sheer and the surf was up. After a nauseating free fall, she hit the water with an icy slap.

The cold was shocking, breath-stealing, but she couldn't afford to freeze up. She started swimming the instant she went under. As soon as she resurfaced, she looked behind her, eyes stinging from saltwater.

Daniela saw only a flash of metal and a glint of bared teeth. Elizabeth was coming after her.

Daniela ducked under again, feeling the whoosh of the blade as it cut through the water next to her ear. Thinking quickly, she scrambled out of her jacket and let it float up, putting a tenuous barrier between them.

Where was Sean?

As if in response to her silent cry, he launched himself off the cliff, his body plunging into the deep like a submarine missile. On his way back up, he grabbed her by the arm, yanking her toward him. They broke through the waves together, gasping for breath.

Elizabeth couldn't swim very fast with an abdominal injury, but she didn't give up. And, despite the crashing surf, a powerful undercurrent was pulling them all away from land, out to sea.

Swimming toward the shoreline was impossible; the waves were so strong they'd be dashed against the rocks. Their only choice was to search for a safer haul-out. The longer they stayed in the water, however, the greater the possibility that a shark would come. Elizabeth and Sean were both bleeding.

That was when she felt it. Daniela didn't think the situation could get any tenser, especially when the madwoman was heading in their direction. Nevertheless, every nerve in her body went taut. The hairs on her arms, which were already standing on end from the cold, practically vibrated with awareness.

Shark.

Sean felt it, too. His face went white. Rather than panicking and trying to flee, he continued to paddle steadily, making no frantic movements. Daniela followed suit, her heart pounding with terror.

The sea in his immediate vicinity was tinged with blood.

"Swim away from me," he ordered.

Her stomach dropped to the ocean floor. Her boots were so heavy, her body wanted to sink down there, too, away from this horror. "No," she said, fury replacing her fear. "No way." Teeth chattering, she sidled closer, until her shoulder was touching his.

Sensing trouble, Elizabeth began to tread water, scanning the ocean around them.

Daniela unbuttoned the shirt she was wearing with trembling fingers and took it off. "I'm going to tie this around your forearm."

He nodded, holding still while she wrapped it tight. "If a shark comes—"

"I won't leave you."

A muscle in his jaw ticked, but he didn't argue with her. In fact, he pulled a utility knife from his belt and held it at the ready. Never mind that white sharks had a mouthful of teeth almost the size of his blade, and the striking power of a semi, rendering their victims too insensible to fight back.

The water around them seemed to sing with energy. She felt an immense presence, an unstoppable force. There was a juggernaut beneath the surface, parting the sea beside them, passing with the speed of a runaway train.

Elizabeth splashed wildly, trying to escape, and the

shark struck. Her body jerked forward, rocketing through the water, twenty feet or more. In the next instant, she was pulled under, into a boil of brilliant red.

Daniela bit back a scream, burying her face against Sean's chest.

"You have to swim away from me," he said, his voice flat. "Head for a haul-out. I'll start thrashing to get his attention."

"No," she whispered, shuddering.

"Dani—"

Elizabeth's body resurfaced, much closer to them. Her eyes were blank and her head was hanging to the side at an odd angle.

She was very clearly dead.

A moment later, a fin appeared, thick and black and menacing, slicing through the surface of the water. Coming right at them.

This time, Daniela couldn't hold back her scream.

Sean put his arm around Dani and tightened his grip on the knife, pointing it at the approaching threat. He'd never been so scared in his life.

The shark must have mistaken Elizabeth for the injured party. In addition to a keen sense of smell, whites had excellent eyesight. More likely than not, the shark had been drawn to her frantic movements.

Sean tried to stay still. He could feel the burn of his wounded arm, and even the seep of his own blood, tainting the water, but it was almost as if he were watching a scene in a movie, one step removed from reality. The pain was a dull throb, entirely manageable. Barely discernible, actually.

Faced with a humongous shark intent on taking an exploratory bite, and a six-inch laceration, he found his thoughts wandering. Instead of the here and now, he was thinking about the more-pleasant, semi-distant past.

His memory conjured a kaleidoscope of great moments. Kissing Dani on their wedding day, grinning at the crowd while they were pronounced husband and wife. Feeling their baby kick for the first time. Touching her last night… making her his again.

No more space between them.

Keeping the promise he'd made, he brought her even closer, his injured arm like a band across her stomach. He didn't want to die, and he certainly didn't want her to die. But they couldn't outdistance a great white.

The shark breached in front of them, jaws gaping. Sean jerked Dani backward, out of harm's way. To his utter amazement, the shark didn't attack. He recognized the scar above her eye; it was Shirley. They all stared at one another for an extended moment, and then she sank below the surface, disappearing in a flurry of bubbles.

The rain picked up, pelting the rippled surface where she'd just been.

After a moment Daniela's stunned gaze met his. They were alive!

He couldn't explain why the shark had spared them. Humans weren't their preferred prey, after a fat-rich diet of seals and sea lions. Even so, it seemed like an impossible occurrence, a miracle of God.

Swimming back to shore took every ounce of their energy. They hauled themselves out of the water, with the last bit of strength they possessed, and stumbled back toward the house, shivering with cold and numb from shock.

They both heard the helicopter the instant before it

appeared at the edge of the horizon. While it hovered above them, preparing to set down, Daniela pressed her face to Sean's soaked shirt and cried.

Epilogue

Daniela and Sean walked toward the gravesite, hand in hand. He did the honors, crouching to place the bouquet near the headstone.

> *Natalie Ann Carmichael*
> *Beloved daughter*
> *Rest in Peace*

It was still difficult for Daniela to visit this place, but less so as time wore on. The harrowing experience at the Farallones had inspired her to appreciate what she had. Natalie was gone, but they were here.

Daniela felt lucky to be alive.

When he straightened, she put her arms around his neck

and pressed her face to his chest, holding on tight. They stayed that way for a long while.

In the weeks since the ordeal, they'd gone back to counseling, working with a female psychologist who specialized in grief management and post-traumatic stress disorder. They talked about Elizabeth, dealing with the aftermath of a violent, shocking end.

Elizabeth's death had hit Jason hard. She'd been a part of his team, his responsibility. He seemed to think he should have been able to prevent the tragedy. Although he'd been in contact with Elizabeth's family, and they bore no ill feelings, he continued to blame himself. Daniela hoped Jason would be able to move on, but she knew better than anyone else that grief was an individual experience.

Her heart broke for him. Jason was like family to her now.

And so was Taryn.

She'd accepted a position at the Marine Mammal Center in San Francisco, rehabilitating injured dolphins. It was a dream job for her, but she seemed melancholy. The disturbing events had changed her, too.

When they'd said goodbye, Taryn had sent them off with lingering hugs and a solemn promise to keep in touch. They'd exchanged a few emails since then, most of them about Brent's progress. After spending several weeks in a coma, he was expected to make a full recovery.

Life on Farallon Island was returning to normal. The Coast Guard had done a quiet, thorough investigation, a new crew was in place and repairs were underway.

Daniela disentangled herself from Sean and pressed a kiss to her fingertips, touching the top of Natalie's gravestone in goodbye.

They strolled down the flagstone path together, hand in hand. It was a beautiful November day, sunny and bright.

She had an important matter to discuss with Sean, an issue she'd been mulling over since they'd reunited.

"Let's walk down to the beach," she murmured, tugging on his wrist. At the base of a long row of steps, she stopped to remove her high-heeled sandals, bracing one hand on his arm. His wound, a reminder of another nightmare they'd endured, was healing nicely.

Carrying her shoes by the ankle straps, she ventured onto the soft sand.

At the edge of the water, they both fell silent for a few moments, struck by the magnificence of the view. San Diego Memorial Park overlooked a breathtaking stretch of coastline.

Sean probably wanted to go surfing.

"I got an interesting job offer," he said, preempting her speech. "Teaching science and coaching the surf team at La Jolla Shores High School. I think I'll take it."

She turned to stare at him, astounded by his nonchalance. "But you love working in the field."

He smiled at her reaction. "You don't want me to consider the position?"

"I would never ask you to make that kind of sacrifice," she said, her heart pounding.

He nodded, sobering. "I know, but I don't really consider it a sacrifice. Just a change. Traveling the world, chasing sharks…well, yeah, it's awesome, but there are more important things." His gaze cruised over her face, assessing her reaction. "I loved coming home to you, Dani, but I'd love staying home with you even more."

Tears blurred her vision, clogging her throat. "Oh, Sean," she said, wrapping her arms around his neck. "There's something I have to tell you."

His shoulders stiffened, almost imperceptibly. "Go ahead."

She looked up at him, moistening her lips. "Do you remember when I asked you not to give me too much space?"

"Of course."

Since they'd been back together, he'd spent every night with her, giving her everything but space. They'd always related well to each other in bed, and now their sex life was more active than ever. He loved her endlessly, almost desperately, as if he was afraid each time were the last, and that she'd retreat from him again.

"I meant…emotionally."

His eyes darkened. "I knew what you meant."

She paused, struggling for the right words to explain her feelings to him. "I know you said it didn't matter if we had children. But I thought you might want to reconsider."

His brows rose. "Do you?"

After a short hesitation, she nodded.

He glanced out at the majestic waves, contemplative. "We're not even married anymore."

She bit down on her lower lip, blinking back more tears. This was so difficult, and not at all like she'd imagined.

Noticing her distress, he squeezed her hand. "When I envisioned having a family, I always assumed it would happen naturally," he continued, his gaze searching hers. "It didn't work out, and I'm okay with that. I'm not going to change my mind, or pressure you into anything. Is that what you're worried about?"

She shook her head, trying to hold the panic at bay. Her hands were trembling, her pulse throbbing at the base of her throat. "I'm worried that I've made a big mistake," she said, taking a deep breath.

His expression became pained. "What do you mean?"

"At the Farallones, I realized that I can't live without

you. And I can't live in fear, either. I can't let my anxieties hold me back."

He just stared at her, waiting for her to explain.

"I had a checkup the other day, and the doctor said I'm fine. Perfectly healthy. There's no reason we can't try again. To have a baby, I mean."

His reaction wasn't what she'd expected. He didn't let out a shout of joy and twirl her around the deserted beach. In fact, he seemed unmoved.

"If you're still interested," she finished, her spirits sinking.

He studied her intently. "Are you doing this for me? Because you think I'll resent you later?"

Earlier, she'd demanded his complete honesty. Owing Sean the same courtesy, she told him exactly what she thought. "No," she said, filled with hope. "I want to try again. For me. For the both of us. I want everything we had before, and all that we have now. I want a family." She paused, casting him an uncertain glance. "There's no rush, of course. Like you said, we aren't even married anymore."

"That's easy enough to remedy."

Her heart fluttered as he got down on one knee. "What are you doing?"

"I was going to do this later, but what the hell." Digging into his pocket, he brought out a black velvet box. While she gaped at him, lips parted in astonishment, he proposed to her, right there on the sun-warmed sand. "Will you marry me…again?"

Tears filled her eyes. "Yes," she said. "Oh, yes."

After he put the ring on her finger, he rose to his feet and she threw her arms around him, hugging him tight.

"I'm ready whenever you are," he said in her ear. "Do you think it's possible to have a divorce annulled?"

Laughing with pure, unadulterated joy, she laced her fingers through his hair and buried her face against his neck, loving him with all her heart.

* * * * *

Harlequin

ROMANTIC
SUSPENSE

COMING NEXT MONTH

Available April 26, 2011

You can find more information on upcoming
Harlequin® titles, free excerpts and more at
www.HarlequinInsideRomance.com.

*With an evil force hell-bent on destruction,
two enemies must unite to find a truth that turns
all-too-personal when passions collide.*

*Enjoy a sneak peek in Jenna Kernan's next installment
in her original* TRACKER *series, GHOST STALKER,
available in May, only from Harlequin Nocturne.*

"**W**ho are you?" he snarled.

Jessie lifted her chin. "Your better."

His smile was cold. "Such arrogance could only come from a Niyanoka."

She nodded. "Why are you here?"

"I don't know." He glanced about her room. "I asked the birds to take me to a healer."

"And they have done so. Is that *all* you asked?"

"No. To lead them away from my friends." His eyes fluttered and she saw them roll over white.

Jessie straightened, preparing to flee, but he roused himself and mastered the momentary weakness. His eyes snapped open, locking on her.

Her heart hammered as she inched back.

"Lead who away?" she whispered, suddenly afraid of the answer.

"The ghosts. Nagi sent them to attack me so I would bring them to her."

The wolf must be deranged because Nagi did not send ghosts to attack living creatures. He captured the evil ones after their death if they refused to walk the Way of Souls, forcing them to face judgment.

"Her? The healer you seek is also female?"

"Michaela. She's Niyanoka, like you. The last Seer of Souls and Nagi wants her dead."

Jessie fell back to her seat on the carpet as the possibility of this ricocheted in her brain. Could it be true?

"Why should I believe you?" But she knew why. His black aura, the part that said he had been touched by death. Only a ghost could do that. But it made no sense.

Why would Nagi hunt one of her people and why would a Skinwalker want to protect her? She had been trained from birth to hate the Skinwalkers, to consider them a threat.

His intent blue eyes pinned her. Jessie felt her mouth go dry as she considered the impossible. Could the trickster be speaking the truth? Great Mystery, what evil was this?

She stared in astonishment. There was only one way to find her answers. But she had never even met a Skinwalker before and so did not even know if they dreamed.

But if he dreamed, she would have her chance to learn the truth.

Look for GHOST STALKER by Jenna Kernan, available May only from Harlequin Nocturne, wherever books and ebooks are sold.

Harlequin®

ROMANTIC
SUSPENSE

Sparked by Danger, Fueled by Passion

SAME GREAT STORIES
AND AUTHORS!

Starting April 2011,
Silhouette Romantic Suspense will
become Harlequin Romantic Suspense,
but rest assured that this series will
continue to be the ultimate destination
for sweeping romance and heart-racing
suspense with the same great authors
you've come to know and love!